Island Adventure
Caribbean Tales

By
Collin D. Butler

Copyright © 2025 by Collin D. Butler

All rights reserved. No part of this publication may be reproduced, distributed, or transmitted in any form or by any means, including photocopying, recording, or other electronic or mechanical methods, without the prior written permission of the publisher, except in the case of brief quotations embodied in critical reviews and certain other noncommercial uses permitted by copyright law.

Published by Hemingway Publishers
Cover design by Hemingway Publishers
ISBN: Printed in the United States

Table of Contents

Story 1:
"The Mystery of the Mango Tree" *A tiny village in St. Vincent and the Grenadines* 2

Story 2:
"The Goat That Loved to Dance" *A village square in St. Martin during Carnival* 10

Story 3:
"Turtle Bay Treasure" *A coral reef near Barbados* 18

Story 4:
"The Talking Breadfruit Tree" *A hillside in Jamaica.* 26

Story 5: "Festival of the Fireflies" *A forest in Trinidad during Diwali* 34

Story 6:
"Calypso Crab and the Big Regatta" *A harbor in the Bahamas* 42

Story 7:
"Sharica and the Jumbie Lanterns" *A sleepy fishing village in Dominica* 50

Story 8:
"The Rainbow Parrot of St. Lucia" *A rainforest in St. Lucia* 58

Story 9:
"King of the Coconut Grove" *A coconut plantation in Grenada* ... 66

Story 10:
"The Stingray's Gift" *A lagoon in the Cayman Islands* 74

Story 11:
"The Calabash Canoe" *A small fishing village in Guyana* 80

Story 12:
"The Ghost Cricket Match" *A cricket field in Antigua* 88

Story 13:
Mariposa and the Lost Shell Necklace *A Beach in Puerto Rico* ... 96

Story 14:
"The Dancing Drum" *A market in Haiti* 104

Story 15:
"The Mango Melody" *Martinique* 112

Story 16:
"The Brave Sugarcane Riders" *St. Kitts and Nevis* 120

Story 17:
"The Anguilla Treasure Map" *Anguilla* 128

Story 18:
"The Starlit Race" *St. Barth's* 136

Story 19:
"The Talking Tamarind Tree" *St. Eustatius* 144

Story 20:
"The Saba Cloud Walkers" *Saba* 152

Story 21:
"Guadeloupe's Glow Fish Mystery" *Guadeloupe* 160

Story 22:
"The Mountain Drumbeat" *Dominican Republic* 168

Story 23:
"The Dancing Conch Shells" *Turks and Caicos* 176

Story 24:
"The Aruba Kite Festival" *Aruba* 184

Story 25:
"The Whispering Caves of the BVI" *British Virgin Islands* 192

Story 26:
"The Secrets of the Baths" *The Baths, Virgin Gorda, British Virgin Islands* 200

Story 27:
"The Dance of the Golden Crab" *The Coral Caves of Cuba* 208

Story 28:
The Volcano's Secret *The Island of Montserrat* 216

Story 29:
"The Friendly Whale of Bequia" *Bequia, St. Vincent and the Grenadines* 224

About the Author
Collin D. Butler

Collin D. Butler is a storyteller at heart, hailing from the picturesque island of St. Vincent and the Grenadines in the Caribbean. A passionate cultural icon and entertainer, Collin brings the vibrancy and authenticity of island life to his creative works. Known for his infectious humor and vivid imagination, he has captivated audiences through his comedy, art, and now, his children's literature.

With a deep love for his Caribbean roots, Collin grew up surrounded by breathtaking landscapes, vibrant traditions, and warm island hospitality. These elements profoundly shaped his storytelling style, inspiring him to create tales that evoke wonder, joy, and adventure. Through his books, Collin aims to share the magic of the Caribbean with children worldwide, sparking their curiosity and appreciation for nature, culture, and exploration.

In *Island Adventures: Caribbean Tales*, Collin masterfully weaves together vivid imagery, unforgettable characters, and heartwarming stories inspired by real Caribbean landmarks and folklore. His ability to transport readers into the enchanting world of sunlit beaches, turquoise waters, and lush tropical forests makes his work a delightful escape for young readers.

When he's not writing or entertaining, Collin is an advocate for preserving the rich heritage of the Caribbean. He uses his platform to celebrate the region's beauty, history, and vibrant culture. Through his children's books, Collin aspires to nurture a sense of adventure and imagination in the hearts of children while paying homage to the land he calls home.

Island Adventures: Caribbean Tales is not just a book; it's an invitation to journey into the heart of the Caribbean, guided by the captivating storytelling of Collin D. Butler.

Dedication

To my beloved Step-Grandmother and Great Aunt, Phemie Davis, and my cherished Grandfather, Kenneth Davis ~

You are the foundation of my life, the pillars of strength and wisdom that have guided me through every challenge and triumph. Your unwavering love, enduring support, and priceless lessons have shaped the person I am today.

This book is a reflection of the stories, values, and dreams you instilled in me, a tribute to your legacy and the unshakable bond we share.

With all my love and gratitude,

Collin D. Butler

Island Adventure Caribbean Tales

Collin D. Butler

Story 1:

"The Mystery of the Mango Tree"
A Tiny Village in St. Vincent and the Grenadines

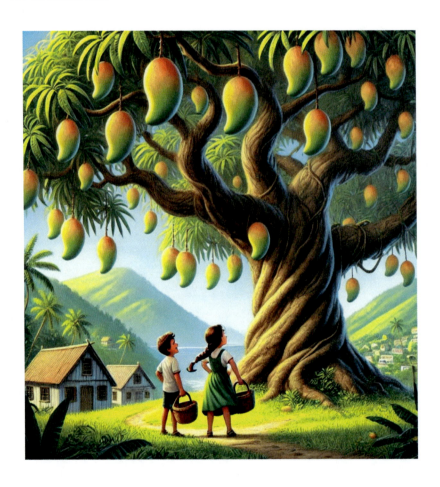

Chapter 1:
The Sweetest Mango Tree

In the quiet village of Gorse, nestled between the rolling hills, a small river and the sparkling black sand beach, stood an ancient mango tree. Its branches stretched wide like a green umbrella, and every year, it bore the juiciest, sweetest mangoes anyone had ever tasted. Jada, an energetic ten-year-old with a thick braid that swung when she ran, loved nothing more than picking mangoes from the tree with her younger brother, Eli.

"Let's race to the tree!" Jada called one sunny morning, grabbing a woven basket. Eli, who was seven and determined to keep up with his sister, sprinted after her, clutching a smaller basket of his own.

When they reached the tree, Jada froze. "Where are all the mangoes?" she asked, staring at the empty branches.

Eli frowned. "Maybe someone else got here first?"

Jada shook her head. "It's too early. The village always waits for the mangoes to ripen properly."

"Then who took them?" Eli asked, his voice dropping to a whisper as if the thief might be hiding nearby.

Chapter 2

The Watchers in the Night

Determined to solve the mystery, Jada and Eli decided to keep watch the next night. They carried blankets and a flashlight to the tree after dinner, setting up a cozy spot beneath its wide canopy.

"Do you think it's a person?" Eli whispered, clutching his flashlight tightly.

"Could be. Or maybe it's a wild animal," Jada murmured, her eyes wide open.

The night was filled with the hum of crickets and the soft rustle of leaves in the breeze. Hours passed, and just as Eli began to doze off, Jada nudged him. "Look!"

A rustling sound came from above. The flashlight beam danced over the branches, revealing a pair of glittering eyes. Then another. And another.

"Monkeys!" Jada whispered in awe.

A small troop of green vervet monkeys were feasting on the mangoes, their nimble fingers pulling the fruit from the branches. One cheeky monkey even tossed a mango peel at Eli, making him giggle despite himself.

Chapter 3
A Plan for Sharing

The next morning, Jada and Eli told their parents about the monkeys. Their father, who was a farmer, shook his head. "Those monkeys are trouble. They'll strip the tree bare if we don't stop them."

"But they're hungry!" Jada protested. "Maybe we can share with them?" she looked at him with big, pleading eyes.

Her father raised an eyebrow. "And how do you plan to do that?"

Jada thought for a moment. "Hmm….we can build a feeding platform in another tree. If we leave fruit for them there, maybe they'll leave our mango tree alone."

Eli jumped up excitedly. "And we can make it fun, like a game! We'll put the fruit high up, so they have to climb for it."

Their father chuckled. "All right. Let's give it a try."

Chapter 4
Monkey Mischief

Over the next week, Jada, Eli, and their father built a sturdy wooden platform in a nearby guava tree. They filled it with sweet, overripe fruits—bananas, papayas, and a few juicy mangoes—and scattered some on the ground to lead the monkeys to the new spot.

At first, the monkeys were wary. They watched from the shadows as Jada and Eli spread the fruit. But by the second day, the troop came closer, sniffing the air. Soon, they were scrambling up the tree, chattering happily as they enjoyed their feast.

"Look! It's working!" Eli cheered.

But not all the monkeys played along. One particularly sneaky monkey, whom Jada nicknamed Rascal, kept returning to the mango tree, stealing the ripest fruit when no one was looking.

Chapter 5
A Deal with Rascal

Frustrated, Jada decided to have a word with Rascal. One afternoon, she waited under the mango tree with a handful of ripe guavas. When Rascal appeared, she held the fruit out to him.

"Here, Rascal. You don't have to steal," she said gently.

The monkey cocked his head, then snatched the guava and scampered back to the platform.

Eli laughed. "Looks like you made a deal with him."

From then on, Jada and Eli made sure to fill the platform with plenty of guavas on the platform, and Rascal stopped raiding the mango tree.

Chapter 6
A Village Celebration

By the end of the mango season, the tree was still heavy with fruit. Jada and Eli invited the villagers to a mango-picking celebration, sharing baskets of fresh fruit with everyone.

The monkeys, now content with their platform, watched from a distance, chattering happily.

"You know," Jada said as she bit into a juicy mango, "I think we learned something important."

"What's that?" Eli asked, juice dripping down his chin.

Jada smiled. "There's always a way to share—if we're willing to try."

Epilogue

The mango tree remained a symbol of harmony in Gorse, where children, monkeys, and villagers alike found joy in its shade. Jada and Eli's clever solution taught everyone that even the smallest acts of kindness can create big changes.

<u>The End</u>

Story 2:

"The Goat That Loved to Dance"
A Village Square in St. Martin During Carnival

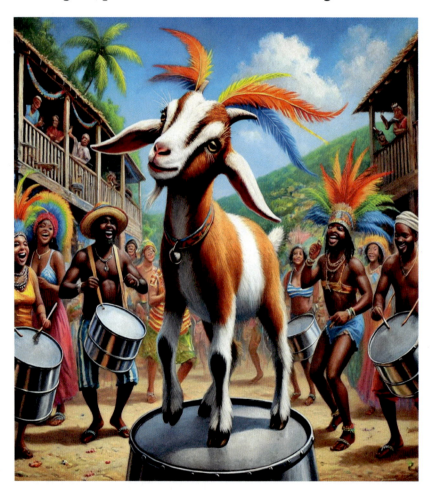

Chapter 1

Rascal the Goat

In a colorful village nestled along St. Martin's sandy coast, Malik lived with his family and his mischievous goat, Rascal. Rascal wasn't an ordinary goat – he had a big heart for adventure and a knack for escaping his pen to wander the village.

"Rascal, not again!" Malik groaned one morning as he found the goat happily munching on a neighbor's hibiscus flowers.

The villagers adored Rascal despite his mischief. The children often laughed at his silly behavior, and the older folk would shake their heads with a chuckle.

This year, the village was abuzz with excitement—Carnival was just around the corner! Malik had been practicing with the steelpan band, hoping to impress the crowd at the parade. But no matter how hard he tried, he still struggled to keep the rhythm.

"You'll get it," his father reassured him. "Just keep trying."

Chapter 2
Carnival Fever

The day of Carnival finally arrived, and the village square was alive with vibrant colors, music, and laughter. Stalls lined the streets, selling everything from roti to bright feathered costumes. The air was filled with the delicious smells of jerk chicken and sweet coconut tarts.

Malik dressed in his simple costume—a bright yellow shirt and matching bandana—and grabbed his steelpan drumsticks. As he left, he double-checked Rascal's pen. "You stay here, Rascal. No trouble today."

But Rascal had other plans. As soon as Malik was out of sight, the clever goat wiggled free from his pen and trotted off toward the square, drawn by the sounds of lively steelpan music.

Chapter 3

The Dancing Goat

The parade began, and Malik's band played lively calypso tunes. Though Malik tried his best, he couldn't keep up with the rhythm, and his frustration showed.

Suddenly, laughter erupted from the crowd. Malik looked up and froze.

There, in the middle of the square, was Rascal, tapping his hooves to the beat of the music! The goat swayed back and forth, spinning in circles and stomping his feet like he was born to dance.

The crowd went wild. "Look at Rascal, go!" someone shouted. Children clapped, and adults cheered, their laughter ringing in the air.

At first, Malik was horrified. "Rascal, stop!" he called. But then he noticed something: Rascal's moves were perfectly in time with the music.

Inspired by his goat's natural rhythm, Malik found his groove. He closed his eyes, let the sweet calypso beats fill his ears, and let the rhythm take over. For the first time, Malik felt as if the music was flowing through him, and his playing was smooth and easy like he was a part of the song itself.

Chapter 4

A Carnival Star

As the parade wound through the village, Rascal trotted alongside the band, his "dancing" hooves stealing the show. The steelpan players couldn't help but laugh and join in the fun, adding playful riffs to their tunes. Malik beamed with pride as the crowd chanted, "Rascal! Rascal!"

By the end of the parade, Rascal was the talk of the Carnival. People asked Malik if they could borrow the goat for future parades, calling him the "Carnival King."

Malik laughed and shook his head. "Sorry, Rascal's got a busy schedule—he's my personal dance coach now!"

Chapter 5

Lessons from Rascal

That night, as the village celebrated with a feast, Malik sat by Rascal, scratching the goat behind his ears.

"Thanks for showing me how to find the rhythm," Malik said softly. "You're not just a mischievous goat—you're a star."

Rascal bleated happily, his ears twitching to the distant sounds of calypso.

From then on, Malik never struggled with his steelpan again. Whenever he practiced, Rascal would tap his hooves along, keeping him in time.

Epilogue

The story of Rascal the Dancing Goat became a Carnival legend, told every year to new generations of villagers. Malik grew up to be one of the best steelpan players in St. Martin, but he always credited his success to his four-legged dance partner.

And Rascal? He continued to charm the village with his moves, proving that sometimes, even a mischievous goat can teach the most important lessons.

<u>The End</u>

Island Adventure Caribbean Tales

Collin D. Butler

Story 3:

"Turtle Bay Treasure"
A Coral Reef Near Barbados

Chapter 1

Kai's Favorite Place

Kai loved Turtle Bay more than anywhere else in the world. Every morning during the holidays, the eight-year-old would grab his snorkel and fins, ready to explore the clear, turquoise waters that sparkled under the sun. The bay was filled with wonders—colorful fish darted through coral gardens, and the seagrass swayed like dancers beneath the waves.

"Kai, don't forget your sunscreen!" his grandmother, Nana, called from the porch. Nana was the best storyteller in the village, and her tales of the sea had filled Kai's imagination since he was a baby.

"Yes, Nana!" Kai replied, already dashing toward the beach with his gear.

Chapter 2

The Mysterious Necklace

That day, as Kai dove near the reef, something shiny caught his eye. He swam closer and found an old shell necklace tangled in seaweed. The shells glowed in the sunlight, and the string holding them together was worn but still strong.

"What's this?" Kai wondered aloud, turning the necklace over in his hands. It felt special, almost magical. He tucked it into his pocket and swam back to shore.

When he showed the necklace to Nana, her eyes widened. "Where did you find this, Kai?"

"In the reef, near the big coral," Kai said. "Do you know what it is?"

Nana's voice dropped to a whisper. "This necklace belonged to Captain Blackwave, the pirate who sailed the Caribbean long ago. They say he hid his greatest treasure beneath the sea, guarded by the creatures of the deep."

Kai's eyes sparkled. "A pirate treasure? Do you think there's more?"

Nana smiled knowingly. "Perhaps. But remember, Kai, the sea only gives gifts to those who respect it."

Chapter 3
The Gift of the Sea

The next morning, Kai returned to the bay with the necklace. As he floated on the surface, he thought about what Nana had said. The necklace didn't feel like something to keep. It felt like it belonged to the ocean.

With a thoughtful frown, he whispered, "I think you're part of the treasure," holding the necklace up to the sun as it sparkled in his hand. "And the sea wants you back."

With a deep breath, he dove down and placed the necklace gently on the coral where he had found it. As he swam back to the surface, the water around him shimmered as if the sea was smiling.

Chapter 4

The Leatherback Turtle

The following day, Kai was snorkeling near the same spot when he noticed a shadow gliding through the water. At first, he thought it was a large fish, but as it came closer, his breath caught—it was a majestic leatherback turtle, its shell as wide as a small boat.

The turtle swam gracefully toward him, its ancient eyes meeting Kai's. It circled him once, then twice as if to thank him. Kai reached out his hand, and for a brief moment, his fingers brushed the turtle's leathery shell.

He followed the turtle as it led him to a hidden part of the reef. There, in a bed of seagrass, lay a cluster of tiny, shimmering eggs. Kai's eyes widened in wonder as he realized they were turtle eggs safely protected by the reef. He had discovered something truly special.

The leatherback swam away, disappearing into the blue depths, leaving Kai in awe.

Chapter 5
Kai's Promise

Kai rushed home to tell Nana about the turtle and the eggs. She listened with a warm smile. "You see, Kai? The sea rewards those who honor its gifts. The turtle showed you something very special."

Kai nodded. "I'll make sure Turtle Bay stays safe—for the turtles and all the creatures here."

From that day on, Kai became the bay's youngest protector. He told the villagers about the turtle eggs and organized clean-up days to keep the beach and reef free of litter.

Every now and then, when Kai swam in the bay, he would see the leatherback turtle gliding in the distance, a silent reminder of the bond they shared.

Epilogue

The legend of Turtle Bay grew in the village, and Kai's story was added to Nana's collection of tales. Whenever she told it, she ended with the same words:

"The sea gives gifts to those who respect it. And if you're lucky, it might show you its greatest treasures."

<u>The End</u>

Island Adventure Caribbean Tales

Collin D. Butler

Story 4:

"The Talking Breadfruit Tree"
A Hillside in Jamaica.

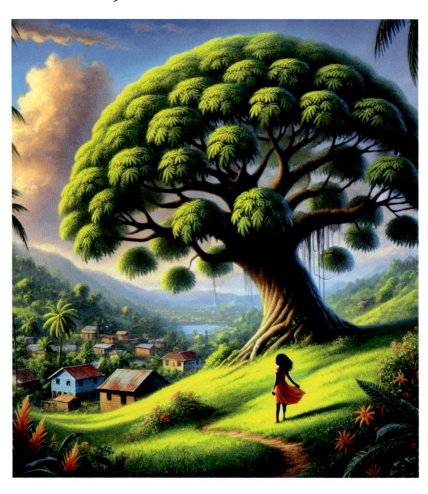

Chapter 1
Grandfather's Tales

Zara loved her grandfather, but sometimes she thought his stories were a little... *far-fetched*. Sitting under the shade of the big breadfruit tree on the hillside, he would spin tales of talking trees, dancing rivers, and singing birds.

"The breadfruit tree can talk, you know," Grandfather said one afternoon, leaning back in his old wooden chair.

Zara rolled her eyes. "Trees don't talk, Grandpa."

Grandfather chuckled. "Maybe you're not listening hard enough. This tree has seen many storms and kept the village safe. If you're quiet, you might just hear its wisdom."

Zara laughed, but the idea of a talking tree stayed with her. That night, as she lay in bed, the wind howled outside, rustling the leaves of the old breadfruit tree. She thought she heard whispers, but she quickly shook it off.

Chapter 2
The Windy Night

A few nights later, the wind returned, stronger than before. Zara couldn't sleep, so she crept out to the hillside, her flashlight cutting through the dark. The breadfruit tree swayed in the wind, its massive leaves rustling like a symphony.

As she stood beneath the tree, Zara froze. The whispers were louder now, forming words.

"Zara," a soft voice called.

Her heart pounded. "Who's there?"

"It is I, the breadfruit tree," the voice replied, low and kind.

Zara's jaw dropped. "Grandpa was right?" her voice, a whisper in the air.

The tree chuckled, its leaves quivering. "I have watched over this village for generations. A great storm is coming, and it will bring heavy rains and winds. You must warn the villagers to prepare."

Zara blinked, unsure if she was dreaming. But as she looked up at the tree, its branches seemed to reach toward her, urging her to act.

Chapter 3

Sounding the Alarm

The next morning, Zara rushed to tell her grandfather what had happened. "Grandpa! The breadfruit tree talked to me! It said a big storm is coming!"

Grandfather smiled knowingly. "I told you, Zara. The tree is wise."

Together, they went to the village to spread the word. At first, the villagers were skeptical. "How can a tree predict a storm?" One man scoffed.

But Grandfather, with his calm and gentle voice, convinced them to take precautions. "It's better to be safe than sorry. Let's secure our homes and gather supplies."

Zara took charge, helping families board up windows, tie down loose objects, and stock up on food and water. The breadfruit tree stood tall on the hillside, its rustling leaves seeming to cheer them on.

Chapter 4

The Storm

By nightfall, dark clouds rolled in, and the wind howled fiercely. The storm hit with a fury—rain lashed against the windows, and thunder rumbled across the hills.

But thanks to Zara's warning, the villagers were ready. They huddled safely in their homes, listening to the storm rage outside.

When morning came, the storm had passed, leaving the village intact. The only damage was a few fallen branches and scattered debris.

Zara and her grandfather walked to the hillside to check on the breadfruit tree. It had lost some leaves but stood tall and proud, its roots deeply anchored in the soil.

Chapter 5

A Village Hero

The villagers gathered under the breadfruit tree to thank Zara and her grandfather. "If you hadn't warned us, we wouldn't have been prepared," one woman said.

Grandfather smiled. "It wasn't just us. The breadfruit tree has always been our protector."

From that day on, the villagers treated the breadfruit tree like a special friend. They cleaned the area around it, made sure it was well cared for, and even held a small celebration in its honor.

As for Zara, she never doubted her grandfather's stories again. She knew that sometimes, the old tales held a bit of magic.

Epilogue

The talking breadfruit tree became a legend in the village; its story passed down through generations. Whenever the wind rustled its leaves, Zara smiled, knowing it was still watching over them.

And in her heart, she knew *sometimes, the wisest voices are the ones we need to listen to the most.*

The End**Top of Form***

Bottom of Form

Collin D. Butler

Story 5:

"Festival of the Fireflies"
A Forest in Trinidad During Diwali

Chapter 1

Diwali Preparations

The village of Tamarin was alive with excitement as Diwali approached. Homes were cleaned and decorated with rangoli patterns made from colored powder. Strings of marigolds adorned doorways, and the scent of freshly made sweets like gulab jamun and barfi filled the air.

Amara, a spirited eight-year-old, was thrilled about the festival of lights. She couldn't wait to see the flickering diyas and the dazzling firecrackers. But her excitement dimmed when her older cousins were given the important job of lighting the diyas around the village.

"Why can't I help light the diyas?" Amara asked her mother, her big brown eyes full of hope.

"You're still too young," her mother replied gently, brushing a strand of hair away from Amara's face. "Maybe next year."

Feeling left out, Amara sulked on the porch. "It's not fair," she muttered, watching her cousins carry the clay lamps with pride.

Chapter 2
The Forest Escape

As dusk approached, Amara decided to escape the hustle and bustle of the village and take a walk in the nearby forest. She loved the way the tall trees formed a canopy overhead, and the soft sounds of chirping crickets and rustling leaves always soothed her.

She wandered deeper into the woods, kicking at loose pebbles and mumbling to herself. "Why does everyone think I'm too little? I can help just as much as anyone else."

Just then, a soft glow caught her eye. She looked up to see tiny lights twinkling among the trees. Fireflies! They danced in the air like miniature lanterns, their golden light flickering against the growing darkness.

"Wow," Amara whispered, her eyes widening as her frustration melted away. A tiny smile crept onto her face, her earlier pout forgotten. She reached out her hand, and one of the fireflies landed gently on her palm, its soft glow lighting up her curious gaze.

Chapter 3

The Firefly Friends

"Hello, little one," a tiny voice said.

Amara gasped. "Did you just... talk?"

The firefly bobbed up and down as if nodding. "We can only speak to those who truly appreciate the light," it said.

Other fireflies gathered around, their lights forming a soft, glowing circle. "Why are you sad?" one of them asked.

Amara explained how she felt left out of the Diwali preparations. "Everyone says I'm too young to help," she said.

The fireflies buzzed thoughtfully. "Light isn't about age or size," one said. "It's about spreading joy and working together. Would you like us to show you?"

Amara's face lit up. "Yes, please!"

Chapter 4:
A Magical Team Effort

The fireflies led Amara to a clearing where their lights sparkled like stars. "Watch this," one firefly said, and the group began to form shapes in the air—a glowing diya, a swirling rangoli pattern, and even a crescent moon.

Amara clapped her hands in delight. "You're amazing!"

"You can join us," a firefly said. "Together, we'll create something truly special."

Amara picked up a fallen twig and began tracing patterns on the ground. The fireflies hovered over her designs, lighting them up with their golden glow. Together, they created a glowing path that led back toward the village.

Chapter 5

The Festival of the Fireflies

When Amara returned to the village, her parents and cousins were lighting the last of the diyas. The fireflies swirled around her, their light blending with the flickering lamps to create a breathtaking view.

"Amara! What's happening?" her mother asked, astonished.

"It's my new friends," Amara said with a grin. "They wanted to help make Diwali even brighter."

The villagers gathered to watch as the fireflies danced through the air, their lights reflecting off the diyas and adding a magical glow to the celebration. Children laughed and clapped, and even the older cousins were impressed.

"Looks like you brought the stars down to earth," her cousin said with a smile.

Amara beamed. For the first time, she felt like an important part of the festival.

Chapter 6:
A New Tradition

From that night on, the villagers of Tamarin had a new Diwali tradition. They would leave small bowls of sugar water at the edge of the forest to thank the fireflies for their light.

As for Amara, she learned that even the smallest contributions can make a big difference when done with love and teamwork.

Sitting on her porch after the festival, she looked toward the forest and whispered, "Thank you, my friends." In the distance, the fireflies blinked their lights as if saying, "You're welcome."

Epilogue

The story of Amara and the fireflies became a beloved tale in Tamarin. Every Diwali, the children would gather at the forest's edge, hoping to catch a glimpse of the magical lights. And Amara, now older, always reminded them:

"Light isn't just about brightness—it's about sharing it with others."

The End

Collin D. Butler

Story 6:

"Calypso Crab and the Big Regatta"
A Harbor in the Bahamas

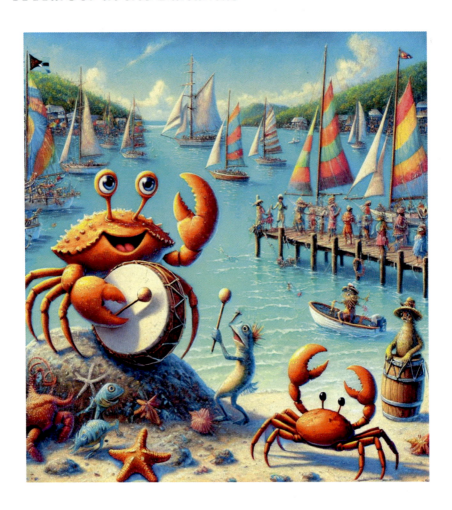

Chapter 1

Sammy's Dream

Sammy was no ordinary crab. With his bright red shell and nimble claws, he was the fastest runner on the sandy shores of the Bahamian harbor. But what made Sammy truly special was his love for music. While most crabs scurried about in silence, Sammy loved tapping rhythms on rocks and clicking his claws in perfect time to the waves.

Every year, the harbor came alive with the sound of laughter, music, and sails flapping in the wind for the Big Regatta. Boats of all shapes and sizes raced across the sparkling water while musicians played joyful calypso tunes.

One sunny morning, as Sammy watched the boats prepare for the regatta, he sighed. "If only I could join in. But I'm just a little crab—no one will notice me."

Chapter 2

The Storm

The excitement for the regatta grew as the day approached. Sammy watched from the rocks as sailors polished their boats and musicians practiced on the docks. But just two days before the big event, dark clouds gathered over the horizon.

The storm hit with fierce winds and heavy rain, battering the harbor. When it finally passed, the sailors discovered that one of the regatta's most beautiful boats, *The Bahama Breeze*, had been badly damaged.

"This is terrible," one sailor said, shaking his head. "The regatta won't be the same without *The Bahama Breeze*."

The musicians, too, were downhearted. Their instruments were soaked, and their stage on the dock had been blown away.

Sammy scuttled to the shoreline, his heart sinking. The harbor, once so lively, was now filled with gloom. "We can't let the regatta fail," Sammy said to himself. "There must be something I can do."

Chapter 3

A Crab's Big Idea

Sammy called a meeting with his sea-creature friends. There was Coral, the sea star; Finn, the fish; and Shelly, the shy hermit crab.

"I have a plan," Sammy announced, clicking his claws excitedly. "If the sailors and musicians can't lift their spirits, we will! We'll form a calypso band and bring back the joy of the regatta."

Coral twirled in delight. "What a fabulous idea! I can make music by tapping shells. Clickity-clack, just like that!"

Finn flipped his fins. "I can hum the melody! Hmm-hmm-hmm, I'll keep the tune going!"

Shelly hesitated. "But we're so small." She whispered, glancing at the big boats in the distance. "Will anyone even hear us?"

Sammy placed a claw on Shelly's and gave her a warm smile. "We may be small, but together, we can make a big difference!"

Chapter 4
The Underwater Band

Over the next day, Sammy and his friends gathered everything they needed for their band. Coral collected smooth shells, Sammy found driftwood for drums, and Finn practiced humming notes that echoed through the water. Even Shelly overcame her shyness, clicking her shell in rhythm with the beat.

By the morning of the regatta, the underwater band was ready. The harbor was still quiet, and the sailors worked quietly on their boats. Sammy climbed onto a rock near the dock and gave the signal.

"One, two, three—play!"

The calypso rhythm began with Coral tapping her shells, Sammy drumming on the driftwood, and Finn humming a cheerful tune. Shelly clicked her shell like a castanet, adding a playful beat.

Chapter 5
Bringing Back the Joy

The sailors stopped and listened. The lively music echoed across the harbor, lifting their spirits.

"It's beautiful!" one sailor said.

"Where's it coming from?" asked another.

The sea creatures didn't stop. Sammy led the band in a joyful tune that made the sailors tap their feet and smile. The musicians, inspired by the sound, grabbed their instruments and joined in.

Soon, the entire harbor was filled with music. Sailors danced on the docks, children clapped their hands, and even the captain of *The Bahama Breeze* grinned.

"Thank you, little crab," the captain said to Sammy. "You reminded us that the regatta is about joy, not just racing."

Chapter 6
The Heart of the Regatta

That afternoon, the regatta went on as planned. Although *The Bahama Breeze* couldn't race, the sailors cheered louder than ever. Sammy and his band played from the water, their calypso beat blending perfectly with the music onshore.

When the final boat crossed the finish line, the crowd erupted in applause. Sammy clicked his claws proudly, knowing that he and his friends had made the day unforgettable.

Epilogue

From that day on, Sammy and his underwater band became a beloved part of the Big Regatta. Each year, their calypso music reminded everyone that even the smallest creatures can bring the biggest joy.

And as for Sammy, he no longer dreamed of being part of the regatta—he knew he was already its heart.

The End

Collin D. Butler

Story 7:

"Sharica and the Jumbie Lanterns"
A Sleepy Fishing Village in Dominica

Chapter 1

The Warnings

In the sleepy fishing village of Scotts Head, life moved to the rhythm of the sea. Sharica, a spirited nine-year-old, loved exploring the sandy beaches, rocky coves, and mangrove forests near her home. Her favorite time was dusk, when the sun dipped below the horizon, painting the sky in hues of orange and pink.

"Sharica, stay inside after dark," her grandmother warned one evening. "The jumbie lanterns come out then."

Sharica rolled her eyes. "Granny, you always say that. What's a jumbie lantern, anyway?"

"They are the lights of mischievous spirits who lure the curious away. If you follow them, you may never come back."

Sharica nodded politely but didn't believe the tales. Her grandmother was full of stories about jumbies, soucouyants, and other magical beings. They were just that—stories.

Chapter 2

The Lanterns Appear

One moonless night, Sharica couldn't sleep. The cool breeze rustled the palm trees outside, and the sound of waves lapping against the shore called to her. Quietly, she tiptoed out of the house, careful not to wake her grandmother, who was softly snoring nearby.

As she reached the beach, a flicker of light caught her eye. It floated just above the sand, glowing softly like a firefly. Then another light appeared, and another, until a string of glowing orbs danced along the shoreline.

"Jumbie lanterns?" Sharica whispered, her heart pounding. A little shiver ran down her spine, but curiosity tugged at her stronger than fear.

She followed the lights as they bobbed and weaved down the beach, their glow brightening the dark night.

Chapter 3
The Magical World

The lights led Sharica to a narrow path through the mangroves, where the air smelled of salt and mystery. She hesitated but couldn't resist following.

Suddenly, the path opened into a glowing clearing. The world around her shimmered as if the stars had fallen from the sky. The trees sparkled with silver leaves, and the sand beneath her feet glowed faintly.

"Welcome, Sharica," a voice echoed.

Sharica turned to see small, glowing figures emerging from the trees. They were no taller than her waist, with mischievous grins and twinkling eyes. These were the jumbies her grandmother had warned her about.

"You followed our lanterns," one of them said, clapping its tiny hands. "Now, you must prove your courage and wit to find your way home."

Sharica's heart raced, but she squared her shoulders. "I'm not afraid," she said, though her voice shillyshallied slightly.

Chapter 4

The Jumbies' Tests

The jumbies clapped and danced around her, their laughter echoing through the clearing. "We'll see!" one of them said, snapping its fingers.

In an instant, Sharica was surrounded by challenges. The first test was a maze of glowing vines. "Find the path that leads to the ocean," a jumbie instructed.

Sharica studied the vines and noticed a faint breeze carrying the scent of salt. "That must be the way," she thought, carefully navigating through the maze.

The second test was a riddle: "What has no legs but can run, no mouth but can roar?"

"The sea," Sharica answered confidently, remembering her grandmother's stories.

The jumbies nodded, impressed. "One final test remains," they said.

Chapter 5
The Test of Trust

For the last challenge, the jumbies gave Sharica a lantern and pointed to two paths. "One will lead you home, and the other will trap you here forever. Choose wisely."

Sharica hesitated, staring at the glowing paths. She thought of her grandmother's warnings, her voice in her mind reminding her to trust her instincts and wisdom.

Then she noticed something—the faint hum of the sea breeze. The same breeze that had guided her through the maze. She turned to the path where the breeze was strongest.

"This one," she said firmly.

The jumbies cheered and clapped their tiny hands. "You have passed our tests, brave Sharica. You may return home."

Chapter 6

A Lesson Learned

The glowing world faded, and Sharica found herself back on the beach. The first rays of dawn painted the sky with pink and gold, like a watercolor painting. She clutched the lantern tightly and hurried home.

Her grandmother was waiting on the porch, her arms crossed but her eyes soft with relief. "You followed the jumbie lanterns, didn't you?"

Sharica nodded, tears welling in her eyes. "I'm sorry, Granny. You were right."

Her grandmother pulled her into a hug. "I'm glad you're safe, my child. Remember, our stories carry wisdom. They're not just tales—they're warnings."

Epilogue

From that day on, Sharica listened carefully to her grandmother's stories. She shared her adventure with the villagers, reminding them of the magic and wisdom in their traditions.

And on moonless nights, when the jumbie lanterns danced along the beach, Sharica stayed safely inside, knowing that curiosity and courage must always be balanced with respect.

The End

Collin D. Butler

Story 8:

"The Rainbow Parrot of St. Lucia"
A Rainforest in St. Lucia

Chapter 1
The Legend of the Rainbow Parrot

In the heart of St. Lucia, where lush rainforests stretch toward the sky and waterfalls sing in hidden coves, lived Amelie, a curious and brave ten-year-old. Her favorite place was her grandmother's veranda, where the old woman wove tales of magic and mystery.

"Tell me the story of the rainbow parrot again, Nana!" Amelie begged one breezy afternoon.

Her grandmother chuckled, settling into her rocking chair. "The rainbow parrot is a rare and magical bird, its feathers shimmering with every color of the rainbow. They say it only appears to those with pure hearts. If you're lucky enough to see it, it will guide you to something precious."

"Something precious like treasure?" Amelie's eyes sparkled.

"Something more valuable than gold," Nana replied. "But remember, child, the parrot is a protector of the rainforest. It only helps those who show kindness to the land and its creatures."

Amelie listened intently, dreaming of the day she might see the legendary bird.

Chapter 2

Into the Rainforest

A month later, a severe drought struck Amelie's village. The streams dried up, and the crops withered under the hot, unblinking sun. Families struggled to find water, and the once-lush fields turned to dust.

One morning, determined to help, Amelie set off into the rainforest, hoping to find a new source of water or food for the village. With her machete strapped to her side and a canteen slung over her shoulder, she entered the dense greenery, her heart pounding with both excitement and fear.

The rainforest was alive with sound—the chirping of insects, the rustling of leaves, and the occasional call of distant birds. Amelie's footsteps were careful as she navigated the winding trails, her eyes scanning for anything that could help her village.

Chapter 3

The Trapped Parrot

Hours later, just as Amelie was about to rest, she heard a faint, sorrowful squawk. She followed the sound and discovered a magnificent parrot entangled in a web of thorny vines.

Its feathers gleamed with vibrant colors—red, blue, green, gold—just like Nana's stories. "The rainbow parrot!" Amelie gasped.

The bird's intelligent eyes met hers, filled with a mix of fear and hope. Without hesitation, Amelie approached carefully. "Don't worry, I'll help you," she said softly.

Using her machete in hand, she cut away the vines, freeing the parrot's wings and legs. The bird flapped its wings experimentally before letting out a joyous cry.

"Are you okay?" Amelie asked, stepping back to give the parrot space. The bird tilted its head, then took off into the air, circling above her.

Chapter 4
The Hidden Grove

Instead of flying away, the parrot squawked and flitted from tree to tree as if it wanted Amelie to follow. Intrigued, she chased after it, weaving through the rainforest.

The bird led her to a hidden grove surrounded by towering trees. In the center of the grove was a crystal-clear spring bubbling with fresh water. Around it grew trees heavy with strange, colorful fruits she had never seen before.

Amelie knelt by the spring and drank deeply, the cool water reviving her. She plucked one of the fruits and tasted it—it was sweet and juicy, unlike anything she had ever eaten.

"This could save the village!" she exclaimed, filling her canteen and gathering as many fruits as she could carry.

The parrot landed on a low branch, watching her with what seemed like approval.

Chapter 5

Saving the Village

When Amelie returned to the village, the people were amazed by the water and fruits she brought back. "Where did you find these?" her mother asked.

"In a grove deep in the rainforest," Amelie replied. "The rainbow parrot showed me the way."

At first, the villagers were skeptical of her story, but when Amelie led them to the grove the next day, they saw the spring and fruit trees for themselves. The spring provided enough water for the village, and the fruits nourished the people, keeping them strong until the rains returned.

Chapter 6
A Lasting Bond

The drought eventually ended, but the villagers never forgot the rainbow parrot's gift. They treated the rainforest with greater respect, planting trees and cleaning the streams to honor the land and its magical protector.

As for Amelie, she often returned to the grove, where the parrot would sometimes appear, watching her from a distance. She would smile and wave, knowing they shared a bond of trust and gratitude.

Epilogue

Amelie's story became a legend in the village, passed down from generation to generation. Whenever a rainbow appeared in the sky, the villagers would say, "The rainbow parrot is watching over us."

And in her heart, Amelie knew the bird's true treasure wasn't the water or the fruit but the reminder that kindness to nature brings its own kind of magic.

The End

Collin D. Butler

Story 9:

"King of the Coconut Grove"
A Coconut Plantation in Grenada

Chapter 1

The Climb of Dreams

The village of Gouyave was famous for its sprawling coconut plantation, where the tallest and strongest palms swayed under the Caribbean sun. Every year, the Coconut Festival brought villagers together to celebrate with music, food, and games. The highlight was the coconut climbing competition, where the fastest climber earned the special title of "King of the Grove."

Aaron, a spirited twelve-year-old, dreamed of winning that title. His older cousins, Malik and Troy, had dominated the competition for years, but Aaron was determined to prove himself.

"You're too young, Aaron," Malik teased, ruffling Aaron's hair. "Leave the climbing to the big boys."

Aaron scowled. "I'll show you. Just wait until the festival!"

Chapter 2
Practice and Frustration

Every morning, Aaron woke early to practice. He tied a rope around his feet, mimicking the technique of the seasoned climbers, and tried to scale the tallest trees on the plantation. But no matter how hard he tried, he couldn't match the speed and skill of his cousins.

One afternoon, after another failed climb, Aaron sat at the base of a tree, frustrated and exhausted.

"Trouble, young man?" a voice called.

Aaron looked up to see an old man with a weathered face and a kind smile. He leaned on a walking stick, his eyes twinkling with curiosity.

"I can't climb fast enough," Aaron admitted, his eyes sad. "The festival is coming, and I'll never beat Malik and Troy."

The old man chuckled. "Speed is not just about strength. It's about balance and focus. Would you like me to teach you?"

Looking at the old man, Aaron nodded eagerly, his eyes sparkling with hope. "Yes, please!"

Chapter 3
The Lessons Begin

The old man introduced himself as Mr. Joseph, a retired climber who had won the Coconut Festival many years ago. Over the next few weeks, Aaron trained under his guidance.

"Feel the tree," Mr. Joseph instructed. "It's not just a pole to climb; it's alive. Respect it, and it will support you."

He taught Aaron how to position his hands and feet, how to save his strength, and how to stay calm when things got tricky. "Don't race the wind, Aaron," he said. "Let the wind race you. Climb with purpose, not panic."

Aaron practiced tirelessly, and slowly, his technique improved. He began to scale trees with a newfound grace and confidence.

Chapter 4

The Festival Begins

The day of the Coconut Festival arrived, and the village was buzzing with excitement. The aroma of roasted coconut and spiced fish filled the air, and the rhythmic beats of drums set the mood.

Aaron stood at the starting line with Malik, Troy, and the other competitors. The towering coconut trees loomed ahead, their ripe fruits waiting at the top.

"You ready, little man?" Troy teased, but Aaron didn't respond. He was focused, his mind replaying Mr. Joseph's lessons.

"On your marks... get set... climb!"

Chapter 5
The Climb of a Lifetime

Aaron sprang into action, gripping the tree trunk with practiced precision. He moved steadily, his hands and feet working in perfect harmony. Malik and Troy shot ahead, their years of experience evident in their speed.

But Aaron didn't panic. He stayed calm, saving his strength and maintaining his rhythm. As the climb continued, Malik and Troy began to tire, their movements slowing.

Aaron's pace, however, remained steady. With one final burst of effort, he reached the top just as Troy's hand grazed the first coconut.

The crowd burst into cheers, their happy voices filling the air like a big, joyful song. "Aaron won! Aaron won!" they shouted. Kids hopped up and down, clapping their hands, while the grown-ups laughed and cheered.

Chapter 6

The King of the Grove

As Aaron descended with the winning coconut in hand, the villagers rushed to congratulate him. Malik and Troy clapped him on the back, their teasing replaced with genuine admiration.

"You did it, little cousin," Malik said with a grin.

The village elder handed Aaron a wooden crown carved from a coconut shell and declared him "King of the Grove."

Aaron beamed with pride, but as he looked out at the cheering crowd, he spotted Mr. Joseph standing quietly at the edge, nodding with approval.

Epilogue

Aaron never forgot the lessons he learned from Mr. Joseph. He became a mentor to other young climbers, teaching them that success wasn't just about strength but also about balance, focus, and respect.

And every year at the Coconut Festival, the villagers would tell the story of how Aaron became the youngest "King of the Grove," climbing not just with his body but with his heart and soul.

The End

Collin D. Butler

Story 10:

"The Stingray's Gift"
A Lagoon in the Cayman Islands

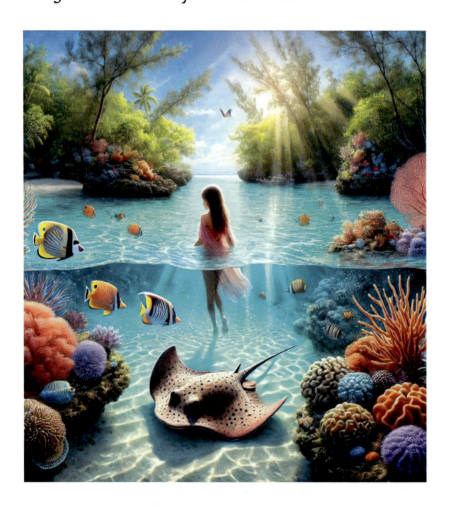

Chapter 1

Tales of the Stingrays

Mila loved the lagoon near her home in the Cayman Islands. The clear, turquoise water shimmered in the sunlight, and the mangroves surrounding it buzzed with life. Mila spent hours swimming, collecting seashells, and watching the colorful fish dart between the coral.

But there was one part of the lagoon Mila avoided: Stingray Bay. Her father often warned her about the stingrays that gathered there.

"Stay away, Mila," he would say. "They're not dangerous, but if you step on one by accident, their sting can hurt."

Mila nodded obediently, but her curiosity about the stingrays only grew. *"They can't be that scary,"* she thought.

Chapter 2
A Surprising Discovery

One sunny morning, Mila decided to explore the quieter side of the lagoon. As she paddled near the mangroves, she noticed something unusual—a small fishing net tangled in the roots.

As she swam closer, she gasped. Inside the net was a baby stingray, its round, flat body flapping weakly as though pleading for help. Its tiny eyes looked at her, and Mila felt a pang of sympathy.

"You're stuck," she whispered.

Carefully, Mila untangled the net, making sure not to hurt the stingray or herself. The little creature flapped its wings, and Mila giggled. "There you go," she said, watching it glide gracefully back into the water.

But instead of swimming away, the stingray hovered near her as if waiting.

Chapter 3

Following the Stingray

The stingray began to swim toward the deeper part of the lagoon, turning back every few seconds as if to say, "Follow me."

"Where are you going?" Mila asked, her curiosity overcoming her caution.

She followed the stingray through the lagoon, past mangroves and coral beds she had never seen before. The water grew cooler and darker, but Mila trusted her tiny guide.

Suddenly, the stingray stopped and swirled around a patch of coral. Mila's eyes widened as she saw what lay ahead—a hidden coral garden, more beautiful than anything she had ever imagined.

Chapter 4
The Coral Garden

The coral garden was alive with color. Bright orange sponges clung to the rocks like tiny suns, purple sea fans stretched their arms, and golden starfish dotted the ocean floor. Schools of rainbow-colored fish darted between the coral, and sea anemones swayed gently in the current.

In the center of the garden lay something extraordinary—a chest partially buried in the sand. Mila's heart raced as she swam closer.

The stingray hovered above the chest, flapping its fins as if urging her on. Mila opened it carefully and gasped. Inside were pearls, old coins, and pieces of jewelry that glinted like treasure from a storybook.

"Is this real?" Mila whispered, her voice muffled by her snorkel.

Chapter 5

A Gift from the Sea

Mila didn't take anything from the chest. She knew this treasure belonged to the sea and its creatures. Instead, she placed a shell she had collected earlier into the chest as a thank you.

The stingray swirled around her in what felt like approval. Then, it led her back to the shallows of the lagoon, where the water was warm and bright.

Mila waved as the stingray swam away, its graceful movements disappearing into the blue.

Collin D. Butler

Story 11:

"The Calabash Canoe"
A small Fishing Village in Guyana

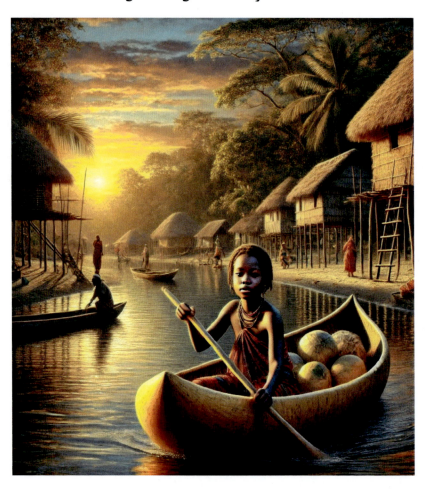

Chapter 1

The Rising River

In a quiet fishing village nestled along the banks of the Essequibo River, Maya lived with her family on a small farm. The river provided them with water for their crops, fish for their meals, and a place to swim during hot days. Maya loved the river, but during the rainy season, it could turn into a roaring giant.

One day, dark clouds gathered above the village, heavy and grey covering the sky like a thick blanket. The wind howled through the trees, and soon, fat raindrops began to fall. The river swelled, spilling over its banks and flooding the fields. Maya watched helplessly as the water crept closer to their house, carrying away crops and leaving the farm submerged.

"Grandpa, what are we going to do?" Maya asked, her voice filled with worry.

Her grandfather, a wise and gentle man who had seen many floods, placed a reassuring hand on her shoulder. "We'll find a way, Maya. We always do."

Chapter 2
The Idea

As the rain continued, the village started running out of supplies. Families needed food and clean water, but the rising river made it impossible to reach nearby towns. Maya's mother worried aloud about how they would get help.

Maya listened and thought hard. Then she remembered the giant calabash sitting in their storage shed. It was the biggest one her family had ever grown—so large two people could hardly carry it.

"Grandpa," Maya said, her eyes lighting up with an idea. "What if we turn the calabash into a canoe? We could use it to move through the water and bring supplies to the village."

Her grandfather stroked his beard thoughtfully. "That's a clever idea, Maya. Let's get started."

Chapter 3
Building the Canoe

Maya and her grandfather worked tirelessly on the Calabash canoe. Using his old tools, Grandpa showed Maya how to carefully hollow out the giant calabash without damaging its tough outer shell. Maya scraped and sanded until the inside was smooth and ready.

Next, they sealed the outside with resin from the nearby trees to make it watertight. They crafted small paddles from wood scraps and even added a sturdy seat inside.

When the canoe was finished, Maya and her grandfather stepped back to admire their work. The calabash gleamed in the sunlight, and its curved shape looked strong enough to brave the swollen river.

Chapter 4
Testing the Canoe

Maya was nervous as they carried the calabash canoe to the edge of the floodwaters. The villagers gathered, murmuring with curiosity and hope.

"Do you think it will float?" one boy asked.

"It will," Maya said confidently, though her hands trembled as she pushed the canoe into the water.

To everyone's delight, the canoe floated perfectly. Maya climbed in, and her grandfather handed her a paddle. Slowly but surely, she guided the canoe through the water, testing its balance and strength.

"It works!" she shouted, her face breaking into a wide smile.

The villagers cheered, clapping and calling her name.

Chapter 5
A Lifeline for the Village

Over the next few days, Maya and her grandfather used the calabash canoe to transport supplies around the village. They delivered food to families stranded in their homes and paddled to nearby towns to bring back fresh water and medicine.

The canoe became a symbol of hope and clever thinking. Villagers couldn't believe how something so simple could become a lifeline in a time of crisis.

"You've done something amazing, Maya," her mother said one evening as they unloaded sacks of rice and vegetables from the canoe. "You've helped the entire village."

Chapter 6
The Legacy of the Canoe

When the floodwaters finally receded, the villagers held a celebration to honor Maya and her calabash canoe. They painted the canoe with bright patterns and displayed it in the village square as a reminder of their strength and unity.

Maya stood beside her grandfather, beaming with pride as the villagers cheered. "Thank you, Grandpa, for teaching me how to build it," she said.

Grandpa smiled. "Thank you, Maya, for thinking of it. You've shown everyone that even in tough times, we can find a way forward."

Epilogue

The story of Maya and her calabash canoe became a legend in the village, passed down from generation to generation. Children would point to the canoe in the square and listen eagerly as their parents told the tale of how a young girl's idea saved the day.

And Maya? She never stopped dreaming big, knowing that even the smallest ideas could make the biggest difference.

The End

Collin D. Butler

Story 12:

"The Ghost Cricket Match"
A Cricket Field in Antigua

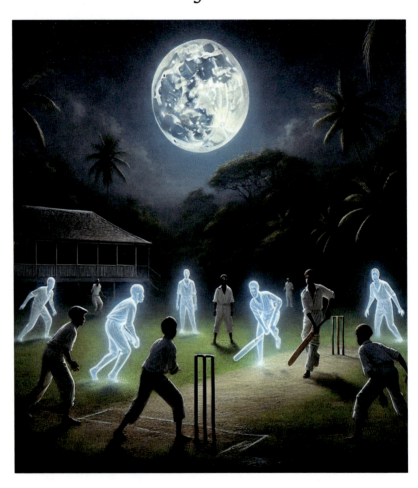

Chapter 1
The Old Cricket Field

In the quiet village of All Saints, Antigua, an overgrown cricket field sat on the edge of town. Legend had it that the field was haunted by ghostly players who never left their game unfinished.

Tariq and his friends, Zara, Malik, and Nina, loved cricket, and they often practiced on a small patch near the school. One evening, as they packed up their gear, Malik said, "You know, the old field is still there. It's supposed to be the best cricket ground in the village."

"Too bad it's haunted," Nina teased, wiggling her fingers dramatically.

Tariq rolled his eyes. "Those are just stories. I bet it's fine. We should play there tomorrow."

His friends exchanged uneasy glances but agreed.

Chapter 2

A Strange Welcome

The next day, as the sun set, the group made their way to the old cricket field. The grass was tall, and the air was eerily still. The field's faded boundary lines were barely visible, and the wooden pavilion creaked with every gust of wind.

"It's... not so bad," Tariq said, though his voice wavered.

As they began setting up, a cold breeze swept through the field, and suddenly, the air was filled with the sound of laughter and the crack of a cricket bat.

"Who's there?" Zara called, gripping her bat tightly.

From the mist emerged a team of players dressed in vintage cricket whites, their translucent figures glowing faintly under the moonlight.

"We are," the captain said, tipping his hat. "Care to finish a match that's been waiting a century?"

Chapter 3
The Challenge

The ghostly captain explained that their last game had been interrupted by a storm many years ago, and they had been waiting ever since to finish it.

"If you win, we'll leave the field to you," he said. "But if we win, you must respect this ground as ours."

Tariq hesitated, but Malik stepped forward. "We accept."

The teams took their positions. Tariq's group would bat first, and the ghostly team took the field. The eerie glow of the ghost players gave the game an otherworldly feel, but the children were determined to hold their ground.

Chapter 4
The Game of a Lifetime

Zara opened the batting, her nerves replaced by adrenaline as she faced the first ball. The ghostly bowler hurled the ball with a speed and precision she had never seen before, but Zara managed a solid hit, sending the ball flying toward the boundary.

The game was intense. Tariq's team scored steadily, relying on teamwork and quick thinking. But the ghost players were no joke – they zipped across the field like lightning, their throws super sharp and their bowling almost magical.

When Tariq's team was finally bowled out, they had scored 75 runs. "It's not bad," Malik said, wiping sweat from his brow. "But we'll have to work hard to defend it."

As the ghost team took their turn to bat, the children realized the challenge ahead. The ghostly players moved with uncanny speed, their bats connecting with the ball effortlessly.

Chapter 5

A Lesson in Teamwork

The children huddled together as the ghost team's score climbed. "We're not going to win if we don't work together," Tariq said. "Zara, your spin bowling is great. Malik, you're fast in the field. Let's use what we're best at."

With a renewed strategy, the children began turning the game around. Zara's sharp bowling caught the ghost players off guard, and Malik's quick reflexes in the field stopped several runs. Nina's wicketkeeping was flawless, and Tariq led the team with confidence.

As the ghost team's last batter stepped up, the score was tied. The final ball would decide the match.

Chapter 6

The Final Play

Tariq took the ball, his heart pounding. The ghostly batter stood calmly, his glowing figure shimmering in the moonlight.

Tariq focused, drew a deep breath, and bowled the ball. It curved perfectly, spinning toward the wicket. The batter swung and missed, and the ball knocked the stumps over.

The field fell silent for a moment before erupting in cheers. The ghost captain tipped his hat again. "Well played," he said. "You've shown skill, courage, and teamwork. The field is yours."

The ghost players began to fade into the mist, their laughter echoing softly as they disappeared.

Epilogue

The children stood on the field, the cool breeze carrying a sense of accomplishment. "That was the most thrilling game we've ever played," Zara exclaimed, her eyes wide with excitement.

From that night on, the old cricket field became a place of legend and pride in the village. Tariq and his friends practiced there regularly, knowing they had earned the right to play on sacred ground.

And whenever they played under the moonlight, they wondered if the ghostly team was watching, cheering them on from the shadows.

The End

Collin D. Butler

Story 13:

Mariposa and the Lost Shell Necklace
A Beach in Puerto Rico

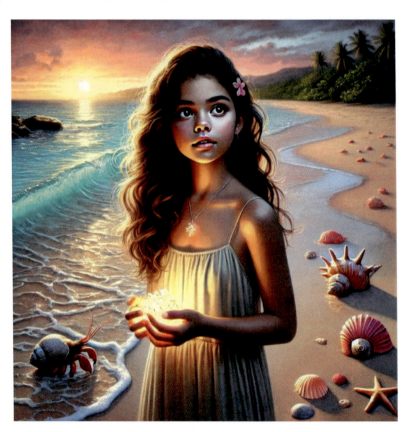

Chapter 1
The Shell Collector

Mariposa loved the beach near her home in Puerto Rico. Every morning, as the sun rose and painted the sky in shades of orange and pink, she ran to the shore with her woven basket. She searched for shells of all shapes and colors, marveling at the intricate designs left by the ocean.

One morning, as she combed the beach, she found something unusual. Half-buried in the sand was a beautiful necklace made of tiny, delicate shells. The shells glimmered in the sunlight, and as Mariposa picked it up, a tingling sensation ran through her fingers.

"It's so beautiful," she whispered, slipping it around her neck.

Chapter 2

The Voice of the Ocean

As soon as Mariposa put on the necklace, the world around her seemed to change. The crashing waves, once a familiar sound, now carried distinct whispers.

"Help us," a soft voice said.

Mariposa looked around, startled. "Who's there?"

She followed the voice to a tide pool where a hermit crab peeked out from its shell. "We need your help," it said, its tiny claws waving urgently.

Mariposa gasped. "You can talk?"

"No," the crab replied. "But you can understand us now. The necklace lets you hear the ocean's voice."

Chapter 3
A Call for Help

The hermit crab explained that a fishing net had drifted into their reef, trapping several sea creatures. "If it's not removed, it will destroy our home," it said.

Mariposa's heart sank. She had seen fishing nets wash ashore before, their tangled threads holding bits of seaweed and broken shells.

"I'll help," she promised.

Guided by the crab, Mariposa waded into the shallow waters of the reef. She could see the net caught on the coral, its threads wrapped around a starfish and a small fish.

Chapter 4
Freeing the Ocean's Creatures

Mariposa worked carefully, untangling the threads without damaging the coral or hurting the trapped creatures. The fish wiggled free with a burst of gratitude, and the starfish moved slowly as if bowing to her.

"Thank you," the creatures whispered. "You've saved us."

Mariposa dragged the net to shore, her arms aching but her heart full. She would take it home and make sure it never returned to the sea.

Chapter 5
The Ocean's Gratitude

As Mariposa walked back to the tide pool, the water around her began to shimmer. The hermit crab appeared again, joined by a group of sea creatures—fish, crabs, and even a graceful seahorse.

"You have done something extraordinary," the hermit crab said. "The ocean has watched over this necklace for generations, waiting for someone worthy to wear it. Now, it belongs to you."

Mariposa felt tears well in her eyes. "I'll take care of it," she said. "And I'll take care of the ocean, too."

Chapter 6
A Lifelong Promise

From that day on, Mariposa became the guardian of the beach. She organized cleanups, taught her friends about protecting marine life, and used her gift to listen to the ocean's needs.

The magical necklace stayed snug around her neck, sparkling softly in the sunlight. It wasn't just a necklace – it was like a little piece of the ocean she could carry everywhere, a reminder of the bond she shared with the sea and its creatures.

Whenever she walked along the shore, she heard the ocean's voice, not in words, but in the harmony of waves and whispers that reminded her she was part of something much greater.

Epilogue

Mariposa's story became a legend in her village, inspiring others to respect and protect the ocean. The beach thrived under her care, and the magical necklace glowed softly as if the ocean itself was smiling.

And as long as she lived, Mariposa never stopped listening to the waves.

<u>The End</u>

Collin D. Butler

Story 14:

"The Dancing Drum"
A Market in Haiti

Chapter 1

The Market's Rhythm

Every Saturday, the bustling market in Jacmel came alive with colors, scents, and sounds. Vendors shouted to advertise their wares, the smell of griot and fresh fruits filled the air, and most of all, the rhythmic beats of drums echoed through the market, giving the place its vibrant heartbeat.

Jean, a quiet twelve-year-old, loved the drums more than anything else. He would sit on the edge of the market, watching the drummers with wide eyes, tapping his fingers on his knees to the rhythm. But no matter how much he wanted to join, he couldn't bring himself to play in front of others.

"You have good rhythm, Jean," a drummer named Papa Jacques once told him. "Why don't you play with us?"

Jean shook his head shyly. "I'm not good enough."

Chapter 2
The Old Drum

One Saturday, as Jean wandered through a quieter corner of the market, he noticed an old drum sitting among a pile of dusty goods. The drum was unlike any he had seen before. Its surface was covered in tiny carvings of people dancing like they were frozen in a happy moment. The outside looked old and a little scratched, but it still seemed strong and tough, like it had a story to tell.

"How much for the drum?" Jean asked the vendor.

The vendor, an old woman with a kind smile, said, "It's not just a drum—it's a dancing drum. If you play it, you'll see its magic."

Jean's eyes widened. He didn't believe in magic, but something about the drum drew him in. He handed over his few coins and took the drum home.

Chapter 3

Discovering the Magic

That evening, Jean placed the drum on his lap and hesitated. He felt silly for expecting magic, but as soon as he struck the drum, a strange energy filled the room.

The carved figures on the drum seemed to glow faintly, and Jean felt his hands move almost on their own, creating a rhythm so powerful that he couldn't help but tap his feet.

His younger sister, Adele, peeked into the room. "What are you doing?" she asked. But as soon as she heard the drumbeat, her feet began to move.

"I can't stop dancing!" Adele laughed, twirling around the room.

Jean's jaw dropped. "It really is magic!"

Chapter 4
The Market Performance

The next Saturday, Jean brought the drum to the market. He wasn't sure why, but he felt like he had to share its music. He found a quiet spot near Papa Jacques and started to play softly.

The moment the drumbeat filled the air, something extraordinary happened. Vendors stopped in their tracks, customers began swaying, and even Papa Jacques started tapping his feet.

"What's happening?" someone shouted, laughing as they spun in a circle.

Jean's confidence grew as he saw the joy spreading through the market. He played louder, the rhythms pouring from his heart, and the entire market turned into a dance floor.

Chapter 5

Overcoming Fear

As the market danced, Papa Jacques approached Jean. "This is incredible! You have a gift, Jean."

For the first time, Jean didn't feel shy. "It's the drum," he admitted, showing Papa Jacques the carvings. "It makes people dance."

Papa Jacques smiled. "The drum may be magical, but the rhythm comes from you. Don't forget that."

Jean's heart swelled with pride. He played until sunset, filling the market with laughter and movement.

Chapter 6
A New Confidence

From that day on, Jean became a regular performer at the market. The dancing drum earned a special place in the community, and Jean's confidence grew with every beat.

He even started teaching other children to drum, showing them that music had the power to bring people together. The once-shy boy became the heart of the market, his cheerful rhythms bringing everyone together. His beats weren't just music - they were like little bursts of joy that made everyone feel like one big happy family.

Epilogue

The story of Jean and the dancing drum became a legend in Jacmel. The market continued to thrive, its vibrant spirit carried by the rhythms of Jean's drum. And though he no longer needed magic to make people dance, Jean always kept the drum close, a reminder of the day he found his courage.

The End

Bottom of Form

Collin D. Butler

Story 15:

"The Mango Melody"
Martinique

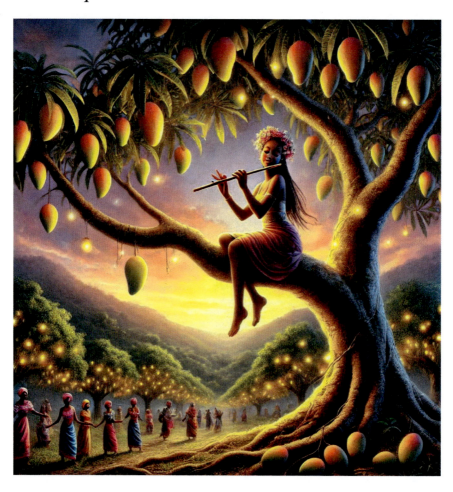

Chapter 1
The Whispering Tree

Lila loved roaming the lush hillsides of Martinique. Her favorite spot was a grove of mango trees near her village. The fruit was always sweet, and the shade provided a cool escape from the tropical sun.

One afternoon, as she wandered through the grove, a faint humming caught her ear. She paused and tilted her head, trying to locate the source. The sound wasn't coming from the wind or the birds—it seemed to be coming from one of the trees.

Curious, Lila tiptoed closer to the tree. Its mangoes shimmered like tiny suns, and the humming buzzed in her ears like a secret waiting to be told. She touched the trunk, and the melody vibrated through her fingertips.

"This is no ordinary tree," she whispered.

Chapter 2
The Hidden Flute

The next day, Lila couldn't stop thinking about the tree. Determined to uncover its mystery, she returned to the grove with a small bag of tools.

She climbed the humming tree, its sturdy branches supporting her as if they welcomed her presence. High among the leaves, she noticed a hollow in the trunk. Reaching inside, she pulled out a smooth wooden flute carved with intricate patterns that seemed to dance in the sunlight.

As she held the flute, the humming became a melody, soft and enchanting. Lila couldn't resist bringing the instrument to her lips. She played a tentative note, and the melody swirled around her, harmonizing with the tree's song.

Chapter 3

A Village Transformed

Lila brought the flute home, eager to share her discovery. She played it for her family, and soon, the melody filled their small house. Her mother, who rarely had time to rest, began to hum along, swaying gently to the tune. Her little brother clapped his hands in rhythm, giggling with joy.

Word of the magical flute spread quickly, and the villagers gathered near the grove to hear Lila play. As the melody filled the air, something remarkable happened. The villagers, who had been busy with their own concerns, began to talk, laugh, and dance together.

Chapter 4

The Ancestors' Gift

An elder from the village shuffled over to Lila after one of her dances. His wrinkly face lit up with a big, toothy grin. "You've awakened the Mango Melody," he said, his eyes twinkling.

"The Mango Melody?" Lila repeated, tilting her head like a curious puppy.

The elder nodded. "Long ago, our ancestors planted this grove to bring harmony to the village. They carved that flute and hid it in the tree, believing its music would remind us of the power of unity. Over time, the story was forgotten, but you have brought it back."

Lila felt a swell of pride. "Then I must make sure we never forget again."

Chapter 5
The Festival of Harmony

Inspired by the story, Lila and the villagers planned a festival to celebrate the Mango Melody. They decorated the grove with colorful lanterns and set up tables laden with local delicacies—Accra, coconut tarts, and fresh mango juice.

When the festival began, Lila played the flute, and the tree's melody joined her, creating a symphony that filled the air. The villagers sang, danced, and shared stories late into the night, their laughter echoing across the hills.

For the first time in years, the village felt truly united.

Chapter 6

A New Tradition

The festival became an annual tradition, with Lila leading the Mango Melody each year. The grove, once a quiet retreat, became a symbol of togetherness for the village.

As Lila grew older, she spent her days under the shade of the big mango tree, teaching the village how to play the flute. She guided their tiny hands, showing them how to make soft, sweet sounds that blended with the rustling leaves. The melody danced through the air, wrapping the children in a sense of wonder. Each time the melody filled the air, it reminded the villagers of their shared history and the power of harmony. Lila's heart swelled with joy, knowing that the magic of the flute and the mango tree would continue to bloom through the next generation.

Epilogue

The Mango Melody became more than a song—it was a bond that tied the villagers together, a legacy of love and unity passed down through the years. And every time the melody played, the tree seemed to hum a little louder, as if singing along with its people.

The End

Collin D. Butler

Story 16:

"The Brave Sugarcane Riders"
St. Kitts and Nevis

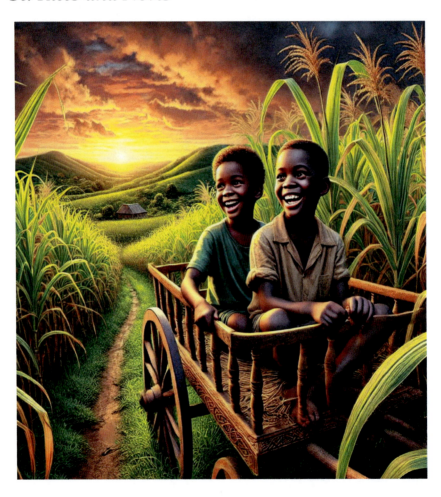

Chapter 1

The Racing Twins

Kael and Kai, ten-year-old twins from St. Kitts, loved nothing more than dashing through the rows of their family's sugarcane fields. The golden stalks stretched as far as the eye could see, rustling like music in the breeze.

"You're too slow, Kai!" Kael teased as he darted ahead, his laughter echoing through the fields.

"Just wait, Kael—I'll catch you!" Kai shouted, chasing after his brother.

The sugarcane fields were their playground, their escape, and their little world of adventure. But one day, their playful races led them to a discovery that would change everything.

Chapter 2
The Mysterious Cart

One bright and sunny afternoon, Kael and Kai were exploring near the edge of the forest when they found something super cool—an old wooden cart! It was tucked away behind some bushes, almost like it was hiding. The cart looked really old, with bits of the wood all cracked, but it still seemed pretty strong. Its big, wobbly wheels were covered in dried-up mud.

"Where did this come from?" Kael asked, running his hand along the smooth wooden surface.

"It looks ancient," Kai replied, examining the intricate carvings on its sides. The patterns resembled sugarcane stalks and waves, symbols of the island.

As they climbed into the cart, a gust of wind swirled around them, and the cart began to creak and move—on its own.

"Kael, what's happening?" Kai exclaimed, clutching the edge of the cart.

"I don't know, but hang on!" Kael shouted as the cart sped forward, weaving through the fields as if guided by an unseen force.

Chapter 3

A Journey Through Time

The cart came to a stop in a part of the field the twins didn't recognize. The landscape looked different—there were no modern roads or buildings, just endless fields of sugarcane and a distant plantation house.

A figure appeared, a boy their age dressed in simple, worn clothes. "Who are you?" Kael asked.

"I'm Elijah," the boy said with a grin. "And this is my home—well, it was a long time ago."

Elijah explained that he was a worker on the sugarcane plantation centuries ago. He shared stories of his life, the hard work in the fields, and the strength of the community that endured those challenging times.

"Your ancestors worked here, too," Elijah said. "They fought for their freedom and built the future you enjoy today."

Chapter 4
The Resilience of the Past

The cart took Kael and Kai on magical trips to the past. They saw women making beautiful baskets, men harvesting cane in the fields under the hot sun, and children, just like them, sneaking little moments of fun and laughter while everyone worked. It was like they were peeking into a world where everyone helped each other and found happiness, even on the busiest days.

They witnessed the island's freedom celebrations, where the community came together to dance, sing, and honor their liberty.

"Everything you see here," Elijah said, "is a reminder of the resilience and strength of those who came before you."

Kael and Kai felt a deep respect for their ancestors and a newfound connection to the land they had always taken for granted.

Chapter 5
Returning Home

As the sun dipped below the horizon, the cart brought Kael and Kai back to the present day. They sat quietly in the field, the weight of what they had experienced sinking in.

"We have to tell people about this," Kael said, his voice filled with determination.

"Yeah," Kai agreed. "Our friends, our family—they need to know what happened here."

Chapter 6
Sharing the Stories

Over the next few weeks, Kael and Kai worked with their parents to create a small exhibit at the local school. They gathered stories from their grandparents, found old photos, and even recreated the carvings they had seen on the cart.

At the exhibit's opening, the twins shared what they had learned. "This is more than just a sugarcane field," Kael said. "It's a part of who we are."

Kai added, "And it's up to us to remember and share these stories so they're never forgotten."

Epilogue

The sugarcane fields of St. Kitts became more than a playground for Kael and Kai. They were a symbol of history, resilience, and hope.

And every time the twins raced through the fields, they felt the whispers of their ancestors cheering them on, reminding them to honor the past and embrace the future.

The End

Collin D. Butler

Story 17:

"The Anguilla Treasure Map"
Anguilla

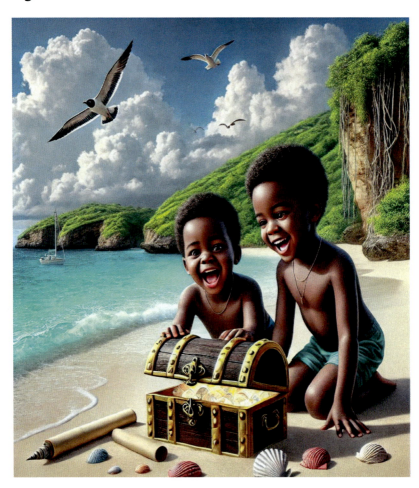

Chapter 1
The Discovery

It was a sunny morning on Shoal Bay Beach in Anguilla, and the waves sparkled under the Caribbean sun. Young Noah, an adventurous ten-year-old, loved digging in the sand and exploring the shoreline for hidden treasures.

"Noah, come help me with the sandcastle!" his best friend, Mira, called.

"In a minute!" Noah replied, digging deeper into the sand. Just as he was about to give up, his hand struck something hard.

"What is it?" Mira asked, running over.

Noah brushed off the sand to reveal a rusted tin box. Inside, they found an old, battered piece of parchment—a treasure map with mysterious symbols and directions.

"A real treasure map!" Mira gasped.

"We have to follow it," Noah said, his eyes shining with excitement.

Chapter 2
The First Clue

The map's first clue read:

"Where the sea meets the sky, and the rocks kiss the waves, find the cave that hides the way."

Noah and Mira headed to the eastern cliffs, where jagged rocks stuck out into the sea. After searching for what felt like hours, they spotted a small cave partially hidden by overgrown vines.

"This must be it!" Mira exclaimed, pulling the vines aside.

Inside, they found a small stone carved with the next clue:

"Follow the trail where the gulls cry loud, and you'll find the treasure beneath the cloud."

Chapter 3
The Secret Cove

The map led them along a winding trail that hugged the cliffs. The cries of seagulls echoed above them as they reached a quiet cove with turquoise waters and soft white sand.

"It's so beautiful," Mira said, awestruck.

Noah spotted something buried in the sand—a wooden chest! Together, they dug it out and opened it with a creak.

Inside, instead of gold or jewels, they found seashells of every shape and color. A rolled-up scroll lay on top.

Chapter 4

The Message

Noah carefully unrolled the scroll. The message read:

"To those who find this treasure: The true riches of Anguilla lie in its natural beauty. Protect the seas, the beaches, and the land for future generations."

Mira picked up a shiny shell and gazed around at the beautiful beach. "It's not gold, but it's more important than that."

Noah nodded. "This treasure isn't about riches—it's about taking care of our home."

Chapter 5
The Beach Cleanup

The message inspired Noah and Mira to take action. They shared their discovery with their parents, who helped them organize a beach cleanup day. Posters went up around the village, inviting everyone to join in.

On the day of the cleanup, dozens of people arrived with bags and gloves, ready to work. Together, they collected trash, removed debris, and restored the beach to its natural beauty.

"This is the real treasure," Noah said, looking out at the sparkling, clean shoreline.

Chapter 6
Heroes of the Island

News of their discovery and cleanup effort spread quickly, and Noah and Mira became heroes in their community. They were invited to speak at their school about the importance of protecting the environment.

"Anguilla is our home," Mira said during the presentation. "If we take care of it, it will always take care of us."

The message inspired other children to start their own cleanup projects, ensuring that the island's beauty would be preserved for generations to come.

Epilogue

Years later, Noah and Mira often returned to the cove where they found the treasure. The chest remained there, a reminder of their adventure and the promise they had made to their island.

And whenever they walked along Shoal Bay Beach, they felt proud knowing they had made a difference.

<u>The End</u>

Collin D. Butler

Story 18:

"The Starlit Race"
St. Barth's

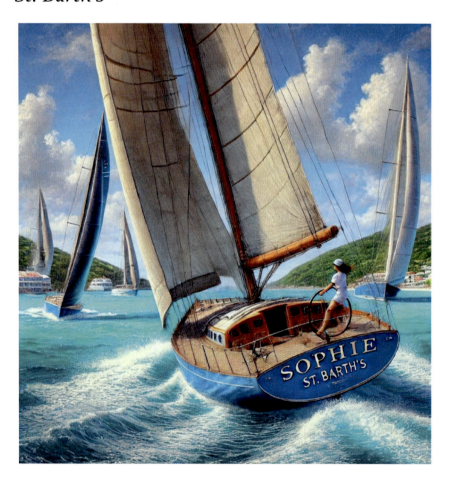

Chapter 1

A Dream on the Horizon

The harbor of St. Barth's gleamed in the sunlight, filled with sleek, white yachts that bobbed gently on the azure waves. Among them, Sophie's boat, *Starlit Wind*, looked small and worn. Its paint was peeling, and its sails were patched. But to Sophie, it was a treasure.

Every year, the harbor came alive for the St. Barth's Annual Sailing Race, a competition that drew sailors from all over the Caribbean. Sophie dreamed of winning the race, but her competitors had modern, fast yachts that made *Starlit Wind* look like an antique.

"You're racing in that?" her rival Pierre sneered, gesturing to her boat.

Sophie lifted her chin. "I may not have the fanciest boat, but I have heart."

Pierre laughed. "Heart won't get you past the first buoy."

Chapter 2

Grandfather's Wisdom

S ophie's grandfather, a retired sailor, had built *Starlit Wind* years ago. It was his pride and joy, crafted with care and designed to dance with the wind. But the years had taken their toll.

"It's a fine boat, Sophie," her grandfather said, running his hand along the wooden hull. "It just needs a little love and attention."

"Do you really think it can win?" Sophie asked, doubt creeping into her voice.

"Winning isn't just about the boat," her grandfather said. "It's about the sailor. Trust the wind, respect the sea, and listen to your instincts. Let's fix her up and show them what *Starlit Wind* can do."

Chapter 3
Rebuilding the Starlit Wind

Over the next few weeks, Sophie and her grandfather worked tirelessly on the boat. They sanded the hull, applied fresh paint, and mended the sails. Her grandfather taught her tricks to make the boat faster, like adjusting the rigging and polishing the keel.

Sophie practiced every day, navigating the tricky currents around the island and learning how to read the wind. She faced challenges—strong tides, sudden gusts—but each time, her confidence grew.

The day before the race, *Starlit Wind* sparkled in the harbor, its deep blue hull gleaming under the starlit sky. Sophie whispered to the boat, "Let's show them what we're made of."

Chapter 4
The Race Begins

The morning of the race was electric with excitement. The harbor buzzed with chatter as the yachts lined up at the starting line. Pierre's yacht, *Sea Falcon*, dwarfed Sophie's boat, and his crew laughed as they saw her.

"Ready, Sophie?" Pierre called mockingly.

"More than you know," she replied, gripping the tiller.

The starting cannon boomed, and the boats surged forward. Sophie watched the wind closely, her hands tugging the ropes as she adjusted the sails just right, like a little puzzle she was solving with the breeze.

The *Starlit Wind* cut through the water, keeping pace with the larger yachts.

Chapter 5

Tricky Waters

As the race went on, the path became trickier. The boats sailed around big, rocky spots and squeezed through narrow spaces. Sophie's little boat zipped and darted, slipping through the tight spots like a playful fish.

Ahead, Pierre struggled as the wind shifted unpredictably. Sophie remembered her grandfather's advice: *"Trust your instincts."* She adjusted her course, catching a gust of wind that propelled her forward.

The final stretch led through a narrow channel with strong currents. Pierre's yacht, built for speed, faltered in the tricky waters. Sophie, relying on her experience and connection with her boat, glided through effortlessly.

Chapter 6
The Finish Line

As the finish line came into view, the crowd cheered. Sophie's heart pounded as she pushed *Starlit Wind* to its limit. Pierre's yacht was close behind, but Sophie's steady hand and determination gave her the edge.

She crossed the finish line first, the cheers of the crowd echoing across the harbor. Sophie couldn't believe it—she had won!

Epilogue
The Starlit Champion

At the award ceremony, Sophie stood proudly with her grandfather by her side. The trophy gleamed in her hands, but the real prize was the lesson she had learned.

Pierre approached her, his arrogance replaced with respect. "You sailed brilliantly, Sophie. Congratulations."

"Thanks, Pierre," Sophie said with a grin. "Heart matters more than you think."

From that day on, *Starlit Wind* became a legend in St. Barth's, and Sophie's story inspired others to chase their dreams, no matter the odds.

The End

Collin D. Butler

Story 19:

"The Talking Tamarind Tree"
St. Eustatius

Chapter 1

The Old Tamarind Tree

On the small island of St. Eustatius, Nico loved spending his afternoons under a towering tamarind tree near the edge of town. Its branches stretched wide, offering cool shade from the Caribbean sun. Nico often brought his books and snacks, enjoying the peace and quiet as the breeze rustled through the leaves.

The villagers often called the tree "the Guardian," but Nico didn't think much of it. To him, it was just a great spot to relax.

"Why do they call it the Guardian?" Nico asked his grandmother one day.

"Because it's been here longer than anyone can remember," she replied with a smile. "Some say it holds the island's stories."

Nico chuckled. "A tree can't tell stories."

His grandmother just patted his head. "Maybe you're not listening hard enough."

Chapter 2

The Whispering Leaves

One afternoon, as Nico leaned against the tree reading, a soft whisper interrupted him.

"Nico…"

He sat up, looking around. "Who's there?"

The voice was gentle but clear. "It's me, the tree."

Nico's eyes widened. "You can talk?"

"Yes," the tree replied, its leaves rustling as if nodding. "I've been watching over this island for centuries. Would you like to hear my stories?"

Nico hesitated but then nodded eagerly. "Yes, please!"

Chapter 3

Tales of the Past

The tamarind tree began its stories. "Long ago, this island was alive with trade. Ships from all over the world came to this harbor, carrying goods like sugar, tobacco, and spices. He stood there, watching them unload and reload, hearing the bustling voices of merchants and sailors."

Nico imagined the harbor teeming with activity. "What happened to them?"

"The island's volcano, the Quill, holds secrets, too," the tree continued. "Many years ago, it erupted, reminding everyone of nature's power. The people rebuilt, stronger and more united, but the harbor slowly grew quiet."

Nico was captivated. He had always seen the island as quiet and sleepy, but now he understood its rich history.

Chapter 4

A New Idea

Over the next few weeks, Nico returned to the tree every day, eager to hear more stories. The tree told him about Statia's role as a free port during the American Revolutionary War. It spoke of ships bringing goods from faraway places, of lively markets filled with traders, and of the strength and resilience of the island's people through it all.

Inspired, Nico decided to share what he had learned. He approached the local museum with an idea.

"We should create an exhibit about the island's history," Nico said to the museum director. "We can show how important Statia was to the world."

The director was impressed. "That's a wonderful idea, Nico. But where will we get the information?"

Nico smiled. "I know just the source."

Chapter 5
Building the Exhibit

With the tamarind tree's help, Nico gathered stories, facts, and ideas for the exhibit. He sketched maps of the island's old harbor, collected artifacts from neighbors, and even wrote down some of the tree's tales.

The villagers came together to help. Some donated old photographs, while others shared stories passed down through generations. The exhibit began to take shape, showcasing Statia's vibrant history and its connection to the world.

Chapter 6

The Opening Day

On the day of the exhibit's opening, the museum was filled with visitors. They marveled at the maps, artifacts, and stories. Nico stood proudly as he explained the significance of each display.

"This is more than history," he said. "It's our story, and we should be proud of it."

The tamarind tree became part of the exhibit, too. A plaque was placed beneath it, calling it "The Guardian of Statia's Stories."

Epilogue

Nico's exhibit became a cherished part of the island, inspiring locals and visitors alike to learn about St. Eustatius's rich past.

And every afternoon, Nico still sat under the tamarind tree, listening to its whispers, knowing that there were always more stories to uncover.

<u>The End</u>

Collin D. Butler

Story 20:

"The Saba Cloud Walkers"
Saba

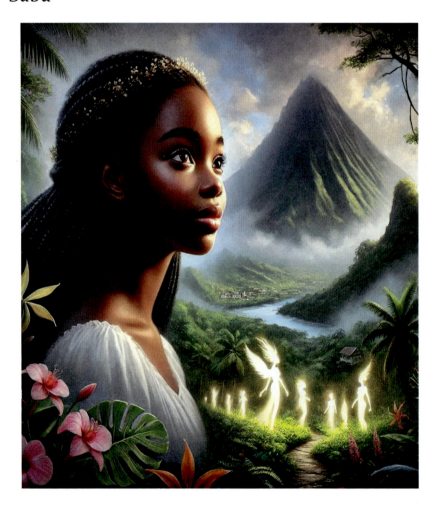

Chapter 1:
Dreams in the Mist

Ella was known for her quiet nature and her love of books. Living on the small island of Saba, she often gazed at Mount Scenery, its peak wrapped in mist like a mystery waiting to be solved.

"Why don't you ever hike the trails, Ella?" her classmates asked.

Ella always smiled shyly and shook her head. She wanted to explore Mount Scenery, but the idea of hiking alone through the dense forest and swirling mists made her hesitate.

"Maybe someday," she whispered to herself as she watched the clouds swirl around the mountain's peak.

Chapter 2:
The Glowing Footprints

One sunny morning, Ella woke up to find the sky brighter than ever. The usual thick mists around Mount Scenery had thinned, and the winding trails leading up the mountain seemed to call her with an inviting whisper of adventure.

Taking a deep breath, she grabbed her hiking boots and a small backpack. "Today's the day," she said, her heart pounding with excitement and nervousness.

As she climbed higher, the air grew cooler, and the familiar mist began to envelop her. Suddenly, she noticed something unusual on the trail ahead: glowing footprints shimmering faintly in the mist.

"What are those?" she wondered aloud, curiosity overcoming her fear. She followed the footprints as they wound through the forest, deeper into the heart of the mountain.

Chapter 3
The Cloud Walkers

The glowing trail led Ella to a small clearing. There, standing amidst the mist, were figures unlike any she had ever seen. They seemed to be made of light and air, their translucent forms shifting and glowing softly.

"Who... who are you?" Ella asked, her voice trembling.

One of the figures stepped forward and spoke in a voice that was both gentle and powerful. "We are the Cloud Walkers, protectors of this mountain and all who call it home."

Ella stared in awe. "I didn't know you existed."

"We reveal ourselves only to those who truly respect the land," the Cloud Walker said. "Why have you come here, young one?"

"I've always wanted to see the mountain's beauty," Ella replied honestly.

The Cloud Walkers exchanged glances and smiled. "Then let us show you."

Chapter 4
The Secrets of Mount Scenery

The Cloud Walkers guided Ella through the forest, showing her the hidden wonders of Mount Scenery. She saw rare orchids clinging to the trees, colorful birds flitting through the canopy, and streams that sparkled like liquid silver.

"The balance of this mountain is delicate," one Cloud Walker explained. "Every plant, every creature, every drop of water plays a role. If one is lost, the others suffer."

Ella listened intently, her admiration for the mountain growing with each step.

When they reached the summit, Ella gasped. The view was breathtaking: the island stretched out below her, the Caribbean Sea shimmering like a jewel. She felt a deep connection to the land she had always taken for granted.

Chapter 5
A Call to Action

Before she left, the Cloud Walkers gave Ella a mission. "The mountain is beautiful, but it is not invincible. Many forget its importance. Will you help protect it?"

Ella nodded without hesitation. "I will. I promise."

When she returned to the village, she couldn't stop thinking about what she had seen and learned. She began sharing her experience with friends and family, urging them to care for the island's environment.

Chapter 6

A Young Ambassador

Ella organized clean-up days for the mountain trails and started a group at her school to learn about and protect Saba's unique ecosystem. Her once-quiet voice grew strong and confident as she spoke about the need to preserve their island's natural beauty.

The villagers were inspired by her passion. Together, they worked to reduce litter, protect endangered species, and educate visitors about respecting the mountain.

Ella often returned to Mount Scenery, hoping to see the Cloud Walkers again. Though they never appeared, she felt their presence in the mist and knew she was carrying out their mission.

Epilogue

Ella's efforts transformed Saba into a model of environmental care. The island's trails remained pristine, its wildlife flourished, and its people grew more connected to their homes.

And on the misty peak of Mount Scenery, the Cloud Walkers watched with quiet pride, knowing their secrets were safe with a young girl who had found her courage and her voice.

The End

Collin D. Butler

Story 21:

"Guadeloupe's Glow Fish Mystery"
Guadeloupe

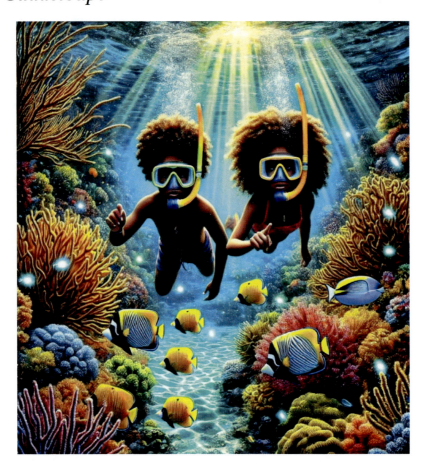

Chapter 1

The Glowing Reef

Pierre loved snorkeling in the vibrant waters of Guadeloupe, where the coral reefs shimmered like underwater rainbows. His favorite spot was near a hidden reef that only he and his cousin Elise knew about.

One late afternoon, as the sun dipped low, Pierre spotted something unusual—a group of small, glowing fish darting through the coral. Their bodies sparkled like tiny stars, illuminating the water around them.

"Elise! You have to see this!" Pierre called.

Elise swam over, her eyes widening. "Glowfish! They're beautiful!"

The cousins spent hours watching the glowfish zip and twirl around the coral, their tiny lights flickering like stars under the sea. Pierre's face lit up with excitement as he turned to his cousin. "We have to show everyone," He said. "This is amazing!"

Chapter 2
The Glowfish Disappear

A week later, Pierre and Elise returned to the reef, eager to show their friends the glowfish. But when they arrived, the reef was eerily quiet. The glowfish were gone.

"What happened?" Elise asked, her voice filled with worry.

Pierre noticed something troubling—pieces of plastic and trash tangled in the coral. A broken fishing net drifted nearby, its strands wrapped around a delicate sea fan.

"This litter must be hurting the reef," Pierre said. "If the coral is damaged, the glowfish won't come back."

Elise nodded. "We have to do something."

Chapter 3

The Investigation

The cousins decided to investigate where the trash was coming from. Over the next few days, they explored nearby beaches and noticed that some areas were littered with plastic bottles, food wrappers, and discarded fishing gear.

"This trash is washing into the sea and harming the reef," Elise said.

Pierre frowned. "If we don't act now, the glowfish might be gone forever."

Chapter 4
The Cleanup Effort

Pierre and Elise began by cleaning up the beach themselves. They filled bags with trash, separating recyclables from waste. But they quickly realized the problem was too big for just the two of them.

"We need help," Pierre said.

The cousins spoke to their school and community, explaining how litter was harming the reef and the glowfish. Their passion inspired others, and soon, dozens of villagers joined them for a massive beach cleanup.

Chapter 5
Restoring the Reef

After the beach cleanup, Pierre and Elise turned their attention to the reef. With help from local divers, they carefully removed the trash tangled in the coral and placed new sea fans and coral fragments to encourage regrowth.

As they worked, Pierre spotted a faint glow in the water. "Elise, look!"

A single glow fish swam by, its tiny light flickering like a hopeful flame.

"They're coming back," Elise said with a smile.

Chapter 6
Education and Celebration

To ensure the glowfish stayed, Pierre and Elise organized workshops at their school and community center. They taught their neighbors about the importance of keeping beaches clean and protecting coral reefs.

Their efforts earned them the admiration of their village. One evening, the mayor of their town held a celebration in their honor.

"You have shown us that even small actions can make a big difference," the mayor said. "Thanks to you, the glowfish are returning, and our waters are once again vibrant."

Epilogue

Pierre and Elise's hidden reef became a symbol of hope and new beginnings. The glowfish returned in greater numbers, their lights dancing through the coral like a celebration of the ocean's beauty.

And every time Pierre and Elise snorkeled in the shimmering waters, they felt proud, knowing they had made a difference for their island and its magical creatures.

The End

Collin D. Butler

Story 22:

"The Mountain Drumbeat"

Dominican Republic

Chapter 1

The Struggle

In a lively village at the base of the Dominican Republic's mountains, the air was always filled with the rhythm of merengue. Carlos, a spirited ten-year-old, loved the music more than anything. His older brother, Mateo, was the village's best drummer, and Carlos dreamed of being just as skilled.

But no matter how much he practiced, Carlos couldn't match Mateo's effortless beats. His hands felt clumsy, and his rhythms were uneven.

"You'll get it one day," Mateo said kindly, ruffling Carlos's hair.

Carlos frowned. "I want to play at the festival, but I'll never be good enough."

"Keep practicing," Mateo encouraged. "Merengue is about feeling the rhythm, not just playing the notes."

Chapter 2
The Journey to the Mountains

One afternoon, frustrated after another failed practice session, Carlos decided to clear his mind. He grabbed his small drum and headed into the mountains, where he often found peace. The path wound through lush greenery, with birds singing and the breeze carrying the scent of wildflowers.

As he climbed higher, Carlos heard a peculiar sound—a steady, rhythmic beating. It wasn't the sound of a drum, but it was unmistakably musical.

Curious, Carlos followed the sound and soon discovered a magnificent bird perched on a tree branch. Its feathers shimmered in shades of gold and blue, and it beat its wings in perfect rhythm.

Chapter 3

The Magical Bird

Carlos stared in amazement as the bird's wings created a melody that resonated deep within him. "Are you making that rhythm?" he asked, his voice full of wonder.

The bird tilted its head and chirped in response, flapping its wings in a new pattern. Carlos tapped his drum tentatively, trying to mimic the rhythm.

To his surprise, the bird seemed to respond, adjusting its wingbeats to guide him. Carlos played again, and this time, his rhythm flowed naturally.

"You're teaching me," Carlos said, laughing with joy. "You're my magic teacher!"

Chapter 4
Practice with a Purpose

Over the next few days, Carlos returned to the mountains, practicing with the magical bird. The bird's rhythms were unlike anything he had heard before—complex yet natural, like the heartbeat of the island itself.

Carlos's hands grew steadier, and his confidence soared. For the first time, he felt the music rather than forcing it.

"I think I'm ready," he told the bird on his final visit. "Thank you for teaching me." The bird chirped and flapped its wings one last time as if giving its blessing.

Chapter 5
The Village Festival

The village festival was the most anticipated event of the year. The plaza was decorated with colorful flags, and the air buzzed with excitement. Musicians gathered to perform, and the crowd clapped and danced to the lively merengue beats.

Carlos nervously held his drum, waiting for his turn. Mateo gave him an encouraging smile. "You've got this, little brother."

When Carlos stepped onto the stage, he took a deep breath and began to play. His hands moved with confidence, creating rhythms that seemed to echo the mountains themselves.

The crowd fell silent, captivated by the unique beat. Then they erupted into cheers, clapping and dancing to Carlos's rhythm.

Chapter 6
The Mountain's Gift

After his performance, Mateo hugged Carlos tightly. "That was incredible! Where did you learn to play like that?"

Carlos smiled, looking toward the mountains. "Let's just say I had a magical teacher."

The festival became a turning point for Carlos. He continued to play, blending traditional merengue with the unique rhythms he had learned from the bird.

Epilogue

Carlos's music became a symbol of the village, connecting the people to the mountains and their natural rhythms. And every time he played, he felt the spirit of the magical bird, reminding him that the best music comes from the heart.

<u>The End</u>

Collin D. Butler

Story 23:

"The Dancing Conch Shells"
Turks and Caicos

Chapter 1
The Vibrating Shell

Maya loved the turquoise waters and powdery beaches of her home in the Turks and Caicos. Every morning, she strolled along the shore, collecting seashells to add to her growing collection.

One morning, she found a conch shell unlike any she had ever seen. Its pearly pink interior seemed to shimmer in the sunlight, and when Maya picked it up, she felt a faint vibration.

Her eyes widened. "What's this?" She wondered aloud, holding the shell close to her ear. A soft, rhythmic hum echoed inside, almost as if the shell were alive.

Intrigued, she placed it in her basket and continued down the beach, unaware that her discovery would change everything.

Chapter 2

The Dancing Shells

That evening, Maya left the shell on her windowsill. As the evening breeze swept through the village, she noticed something strange—the conch shell began to quiver and shift.

Suddenly, it spun in a small circle, the vibrations creating a soft melody. Maya's eyes widened in astonishment. "It's dancing!" she whispered with her hands on her cheeks.

She ran to fetch her father, but by the time they returned, the shell was still.

"You've got quite the imagination," her father said with a chuckle.

But Maya knew what she had seen. Determined to uncover the shell's secret, she decided to take it back to the beach the next morning.

Chapter 3

The Secret of the Shells

At sunrise, Maya returned to the shore and held the shell in her hands. "What are you trying to tell me?" she asked.

A sudden gust of wind whipped through the air, and the shell began to hum and vibrate once more. Maya noticed the wind carrying her toward a small cove she had never explored before.

As she stepped into the cove, she gasped. Dozens of conch shells lay scattered on the sand, each glowing faintly. When the breeze swept through, they began to move, spinning and dancing in unison, creating a mesmerizing melody.

One shell in particular seemed to speak to her, its vibrations forming words in her mind. "We are the guardians of the sea," it said. "The ocean's health is in danger, and we need your help."

Chapter 4
A Call to Action

Maya listened intently as the shells explained. Litter from the beaches and harmful fishing practices were damaging the coral reefs and endangering marine life. The shells had been resting for a long time, but now they were waking up, hoping to find someone who could help.

"I'll help," Maya promised. "What can I do?"

"Start with your village," the shell advised. "Teach them to respect the sea and protect its treasures."

Maya left the cove with a newfound sense of purpose.

Chapter 5

Inspiring the Village

Back in the village, Maya gathered her neighbors and told them about the enchanted shells and their message. At first, some were skeptical, but Maya's passion and determination convinced them to listen.

She organized beach cleanups, taught children about the importance of keeping the shores and reefs clean, and worked with fishermen to use sustainable practices.

One evening, as the villagers cleaned the beach, Maya brought them to the cove. The dancing shells performed their magical melody, leaving everyone in awe.

"The ocean is alive," Maya said. "And it's up to us to keep it that way."

Chapter 6
The Sea's Gratitude

Over time, the village transformed. The beaches were spotless, the reefs began to recover, and marine life returned in abundance. The enchanted conch shells stopped dancing, their purpose fulfilled, but Maya knew they were still watching.

On her morning walks, Maya sometimes heard a faint hum from her conch shell, a reminder of the promise she had made to the sea.

Epilogue

Maya became a symbol of hope and action in her village, inspiring others to respect the ocean and its treasures. And though the dancing conch shells grew still, their story continued to echo in the waves, carried by the wind to those who would listen.

*** The End ***

Collin D. Butler

Story 24:

"The Aruba Kite Festival"

Aruba

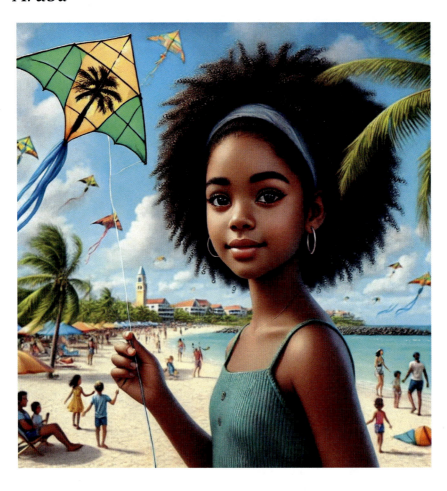

Chapter 1
A Dream on the Wind

In the sunny town of Oranjestad, Aruba, the annual kite festival was the most exciting event of the year. The skies would be filled with colorful kites of all shapes and sizes, and the entire island would gather to celebrate.

Amira, a ten-year-old girl with boundless imagination, dreamed of winning the festival. "This year, I'll make the best kite anyone has ever seen!" she declared to her grandfather.

Her grandfather, a wise and gentle man who had built many kites in his youth, chuckled. "Winning isn't just about making the best kite, Amira. It's about putting your heart into it."

Amira nodded eagerly. "Then I'll build a kite that shows how much I love our island!"

Chapter 2
The Divi Divi Kite

Amira and her grandfather spent weeks designing the kite. Amira wanted it to look like Aruba's iconic Divi Divi tree, which always leaned gracefully with the trade winds.

"Divi Divi trees are strong and unique, just like Aruba," her grandfather said as he helped her sketch the design.

Together, they built the kite using bamboo, colorful fabric, and string. Amira painted the fabric with greens and browns to resemble the tree's branches and leaves. The final touch was a bright blue tail to represent the Caribbean Sea.

When they finished, Amira stood back and admired their creation. "It's perfect!" she said, her heart swelling with pride.

Chapter 3

The Festival Begins

The day of the festival was bright and breezy, perfect for kite flying. Families gathered on the beach, their laughter mingling with the sound of waves.

Amira carried her kite carefully, her grandfather walking beside her. Other children gasped at the sight of her Divi Divi kite, its unique shape standing out among the traditional diamond and box kites.

When the competition began, Amira launched her kite into the air. The wind caught it immediately, and the kite soared higher and higher, its tail shimmering in the sunlight.

The crowd cheered. "Look at that kite! It's beautiful!"

Amira's heart felt like it might burst with happiness as she watched her kite twirl and swoop in the big, blue sky.

Chapter 4
The String Breaks

As the wind grew stronger, Amira tightened her grip on the string. But suddenly, a powerful gust snapped the string, and the kite broke free.

"No!" Amira cried as the Divi Divi kite soared away.

The crowd watched in stunned silence as the kite drifted higher, carried by the wind over the beach and out toward the sea.

Amira felt tears prick her eyes. "It's gone," she whispered.

Her grandfather placed a comforting hand on her shoulder. "Sometimes, when we let go, beautiful things happen."

Chapter 5

A Symbol of Freedom

To everyone's amazement, the kite didn't fall. It floated gracefully, its shape visible against the blue sky. The crowd began to clap and cheer, their voices filled with awe.

"Look at it, go!" someone shouted. "It's like it's alive!"

Amira wiped her tears and smiled as she saw the joy her kite brought to the festivalgoers. It became a symbol of freedom and creativity, reminding everyone of Aruba's enduring spirit.

Chapter 6

A New Tradition

The next day, Amira's kite was spotted caught in the branches of a Divi Divi tree near the beach. The villagers carefully retrieved it and brought it back to her.

"You've inspired us all," the festival organizer said, handing the kite to Amira. "This kite represents everything we love about Aruba."

From that year on, the kite festival added a special category for kites that celebrated Aruba's culture and beauty, inspired by Amira's creation.

Epilogue

Amira never won a trophy for her kite, but she won something far greater—the hearts of her island. Every time she saw a Divi Divi tree swaying in the wind, she thought of her kite and the joy it had brought to her community.

And every year at the festival, kites shaped like Divi Divi trees filled the sky, a tribute to the girl who turned her dream into a symbol of Aruba's spirit.

The End

Collin D. Butler

Story 25:

"The Whispering Caves of the BVI"
British Virgin Islands

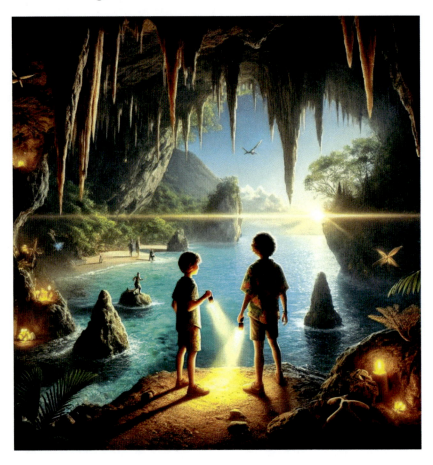

Chapter 1

The Legend of the Caves

In a small village on Tortola, British Virgin Islands, twelve-year-old Anya loved hearing her grandmother's tales about the Whispering Caves. According to legend, the caves could grant a single wish to those brave enough to venture inside, but only if they showed kindness and courage.

"Many have tried, but only the worthy hear the whispers," her grandmother said with a twinkle in her eye.

Anya dreamed of exploring the caves, but the thought of entering the dark, mysterious caverns sent shivers down her spine.

Chapter 2
The Storm's Aftermath

One night, a powerful storm lashed the island, leaving behind broken trees, debris, and rising waters. The villagers banded together to clean up, but Anya's best friend, Kai, discovered something remarkable the next morning: the storm had unearthed the entrance to the Whispering Caves, hidden behind a thicket near the shore.

"You've always wanted to find it!" Kai exclaimed.

Anya hesitated but knew this was her chance. Together, they decided to explore the caves.

Chapter 3
Entering the Unknown

Armed with flashlights and courage, Anya and Kai stepped into the caves. The air was cool and damp, and their footsteps echoed softly. Stalactites hung from the ceiling, glistening like crystals in the faint light.

As they ventured deeper, Anya thought she heard whispers, soft and melodic, like the ocean breeze carrying secrets. "Do you hear that?" she asked, her voice trembling.

Kai nodded. "It's like... they're calling to us."

The whispers grew louder, guiding them through winding tunnels.

Chapter 4
The Test of Kindness

Finally, the pair reached a chamber filled with shimmering pools and glowing rocks. In the center stood a statue of a wise old turtle, the guardian of the caves. Suddenly, a voice echoed around them.

"Only those with pure hearts may make a wish. Show me your kindness."

Anya and Kai glanced at each other, unsure of what to do. Then, they noticed a small crab trapped under a fallen rock near the edge of the pool. Carefully, they worked together to free it, setting it gently into the water.

The chamber glowed brighter, and the voice spoke again. "You have passed the test. Speak your wish."

Chapter 5

A Wish for the Island

Anya thought about wishing something just for herself—maybe courage or adventure—but then she remembered the storm and the struggles of her village.

"I wish for our island to heal and for our people to thrive," she said.

The chamber filled with a dazzling light, and the whispers grew into a joyful melody. "Your wish is worthy. It shall be done."

Chapter 6
A Brighter Tomorrow

When Anya and Kai returned to the village, they found something extraordinary: the fallen trees and debris had disappeared, replaced by vibrant greenery and blooming flowers. The ocean sparkled like never before, and the villagers seemed happier and more hopeful.

"You did this," Kai whispered.

Anya smiled, feeling a sense of pride and wonder. She knew the caves had given her more than just a wish—they had shown her the power of selflessness and bravery.

Epilogue

The Whispering Caves became a treasured secret for Anya and Kai, a reminder of the beauty and magic of the British Virgin Islands. And though the caves remained hidden, the whispers carried on, waiting for the next kind and courageous soul to find them.

*** The End***

Collin D. Butler

Story 26:

"The Secrets of the Baths"
The Baths, Virgin Gorda, British Virgin Islands

Chapter 1

Exploring the Unknown

Twelve-year-old Liam had always been fascinated by the Baths, a labyrinth of giant granite boulders and secret caves on the island of Virgin Gorda. He and his sister Maya spent their weekends climbing the rocks, splashing in tide pools, and imagining the stories hidden in the ancient stones.

One sunny morning, their mother packed a picnic and dropped them off near the entrance. "Stay together, and don't wander too far," she said with a smile.

"Of course, Mom," Maya promised. But Liam, always the adventurous one, had a gleam in his eye.

Chapter 2
The Carved Map

As the siblings wandered through the boulders, Liam noticed something unusual. On one of the rocks near a small cave, faint carvings formed a pattern.

"Look!" he exclaimed. "It's a map!"

Maya squinted. "It could just be old scratches."

"No, it's a map," Liam insisted. "It starts here and leads... there!" He pointed toward a shadowy crack between two massive rocks.

Despite Maya's hesitation, Liam convinced her to follow the map. They crawled through narrow passages, climbed slippery rocks, and waded through shallow pools until they reached a hidden chamber lit by a beam of sunlight filtering through the boulders.

Chapter 3

The Hidden Chamber

The chamber was unlike anything they had seen. The walls sparkled as if covered with tiny gems, and in the center stood a small stone pedestal. Sitting on top of it was an old conch shell that seemed to glow softly like it was sprinkled with magic.

Liam's eyes widened as he leaned closer, his hand trembling with excitement. "Whoa," Liam whispered, his fingers inching toward the shell like it was calling to him.

"Wait!" Maya grabbed his arm, her heart racing. Her eyes darted around the sparkling chamber. "What if it's a trap?"

But Liam couldn't resist. As his fingers brushed the shell, a soft hum filled the chamber, and the sunlight grew brighter. Suddenly, a voice echoed through the room.

"Welcome, young adventurers," it said. "You have found the Heart of the Baths."

Chapter 4

The Spirit of the Baths

The glowing shell floated into the air, and the shimmering walls seemed to ripple like water. A figure appeared—a glowing, ethereal woman who seemed to be made of light and ocean spray.

"I am the Guardian of the Baths," she said. "For centuries, this place has protected the secrets of the sea and the stories of this island. Only those with pure intentions may hear them."

"We didn't mean to disturb anything," Maya said quickly. "We were just exploring."

"And you have done well," the Guardian replied. "But to learn the secrets, you must first prove your respect for nature."

Chapter 5

The Test

The chamber began to change. The sparkling walls dimmed, and the sound of rushing water echoed around them. "The Baths are not just stones and water," the Guardian said. "They are alive. Protect them, and they will protect you."

The siblings found themselves back outside, standing at the edge of a tide pool filled with tiny fish and coral. The Guardian's voice spoke again.

"Your task is simple: Clean this place of harm."

Liam and Maya looked around and saw bits of trash—plastic wrappers, bottle caps, and other debris washed up by the tide. Without hesitation, they began collecting the trash, carefully removing it from the water and rocks.

As they worked, the tide pool seemed to glow brighter, and the fish swam more freely.

Chapter 6

The Reward

When they finished, the Guardian reappeared, her light reflecting off the water. "You have shown care and respect for this place. The Baths will now share their stories with you."

She handed Liam the glowing shell. "Listen closely," she said.

Liam and Maya held the shell to their ears and heard whispers of the past—stories of sailors who found refuge in the Baths, of ancient sea creatures that once swam in the hidden pools, and of the island's enduring beauty.

"You are now keepers of these stories," the Guardian said. "Share them wisely, and always protect the magic of the Baths."

Epilogue

Liam and Maya returned to their mother, eager to share their adventure. They never told anyone about the glowing shell or the Guardian, but they made it their mission to keep the Baths clean and teach others to respect its beauty.

From that day on, the Baths became more than just a playground—it was a place of wonder, history, and magic that they vowed to protect forever.

<u>The End</u>

Collin D. Butler

Story 27:

"The Dance of the Golden Crab"
The Coral Caves of Cuba

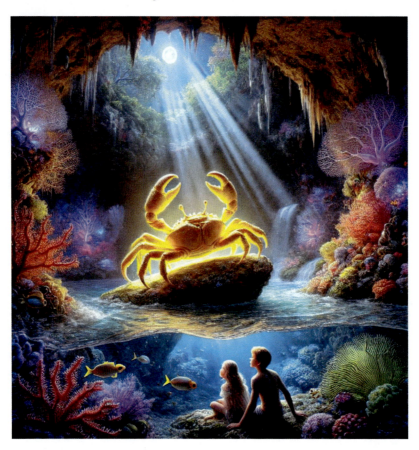

Chapter 1

The Legend of the Golden Crab

On the southern coast of Cuba, nestled among white sandy beaches and swaying palm trees, was a small fishing village. Here lived Emilio, a spirited boy with an insatiable curiosity for the world around him. Every evening, after the day's fishing boats returned, Emilio loved to gather around the village elders to hear their stories.

One tale always stood out to him—*the legend of the Golden Crab*. The elders claimed this mystical creature lived deep within the coral caves beneath the ocean. The Golden Crab, they said, could perform a magical dance under the light of the full moon during the summer solstice. This dance was believed to bring prosperity and happiness to anyone who witnessed it.

"But beware," one elder always warned. "The crab is sneaky and will only reveal itself to those who are brave, true, and adventurous."

As the summer solstice approached, Emilio couldn't shake the idea of finding the Golden Crab. This year, he decided, he would be the one to discover its magic.

Chapter 2
Preparing for the Quest

The day before the solstice, Emilio shared his plan with his best friend, Clara. Clara, a fearless swimmer with a knack for adventure, immediately agreed to join him. Together, they prepared for the journey.

Emilio packed his fishing net, a jar for collecting fireflies to light their way, and a small wooden boat they called *La Estrella*. Clara brought her grandmother's old compass, which she claimed always pointed toward hidden treasures.

As the sun set, bathing the village in hues of orange and pink, Emilio and Clara pushed *La Estrella* into the water. They paddled out under the glowing moon, their hearts racing with excitement and just a hint of nervousness.

Chapter 3

The Golden Glow

The sea was calm and shimmering as if the ocean itself was encouraging them on their quest. Emilio and Clara paddled until they reached the coral reef. The moment they arrived, they spotted a faint golden glow stemming from the water below.

"That must be it!" Emilio whispered, his voice barely containing his excitement.

Clara nodded, her eyes sparkling with anticipation. Without hesitation, they dove into the warm, clear water. The golden light grew brighter as they swam closer to the reef, weaving through colorful coral and curious fish.

Finally, they reached the entrance of a cave where the light was strongest. Inside, they saw it—a magnificent Golden Crab with glowing patterns on its glistening shell. It stood atop a rock, motionless, as if waiting for them.

Chapter 4
The Magical Dance

As Emilio and Clara held their breath, the Golden Crab began to move. Its claws clicked rhythmically, and its legs tapped the rock with precision. Soon, it was performing a mesmerizing dance. The cave lit up with swirling colors of gold, blue, and green, casting a magical glow on the coral walls.

Emilio and Clara were entranced. The crab's dance seemed to tell a story—a story of the ocean's mysteries, the courage to explore, and the bonds of friendship.

After several minutes, the crab stopped and scurried over to Emilio. With one of its glowing claws, it gently placed a small golden shell at his feet. Emilio picked it up, his eyes wide with wonder as he admired the delicate carvings of waves and stars etched into its surface. Before they could say a word, the crab disappeared into the depths of the cave, leaving them in awe.

Chapter 5
The Gift of Prosperity

Emilio and Clara returned to the surface, clutching the golden shell. As they paddled back to the village under the moonlight, they couldn't stop talking about what they had seen.

When they reached the shore, they showed the shell to the elders. The elders gasped in amazement. The carvings on the shell told a story of bravery, friendship, and the magic of the ocean. They declared that Emilio and Clara's discovery would bring blessings to the village.

From that day forward, the village prospered. Fishermen's nets were always full, the crops grew abundantly, and the villagers were happier than ever. Emilio and Clara became local heroes, and their story of the Golden Crab was told to children across Cuba.

Chapter 6
A Memory to Treasure

As the years passed, Emilio and Clara often returned to the coral reef, hoping to see the Golden Crab again. Though the magical creature never reappeared, the memory of that night remained etched in their hearts.

Emilio kept the golden shell on a shelf in his room, a constant reminder of their courage and the magical bond they had shared. And whenever villagers told the story of the Golden Crab, they would smile, knowing that the real magic lay not just in the crab's dance but in the spirit of adventure and the power of friendship.

<u>The End</u>

Island Adventure Caribbean Tales

Collin D. Butler

Story 28:

The Volcano's Secret

The Island of Montserrat

Chapter 1

The Ashy Mystery

Nestled in the emerald-green hills of Montserrat, a small village named Salem bustled with activity. The people of Salem lived in harmony with their surroundings despite the imposing shadow of Soufrière Hills, the island's still-active volcano. Though the volcano was quiet for now, its smoky past loomed large in the minds of the villagers.

Among them was a curious boy named Daniel. Daniel loved the island's rugged beauty—the way the sea waves crashed against black volcanic rocks, the way the lush forests buzzed with life, and, most of all, the mystery surrounding the volcano. He often hiked the lower slopes of Soufrière Hills, collecting shiny black volcanic stones and imagining stories about the island's fiery past.

One afternoon, while playing near a stream, Daniel found an unusual rock. It was smooth, shiny, and unlike any volcanic stone he had seen before. But what intrigued him most was the faint symbol etched into its surface: a spiral surrounded by tiny dots. Excited, Daniel ran to his best friend, Leila, who lived in a house overlooking the cliffs.

"Look what I found!" Daniel said, holding out the strange stone.

Leila examined it closely, her dark eyes widening. "I've seen this before!" she exclaimed. "There's a carving just like it on the old stone wall near the abandoned village. My grandfather says it's a sign of something hidden deep inside the volcano."

The abandoned village she mentioned was Plymouth, once the capital of Montserrat, now buried in ash and memories after the volcano's eruption years ago. Daniel and Leila decided to investigate, eager to uncover the truth behind the mysterious symbol.

Chapter 2

Journey into the Past

The next morning, armed with flashlights, a backpack of supplies, and Leila's trusty dog, Tiko, the two friends set off toward Plymouth. The air grew quiet as they entered the ruins, a haunting landscape of ash-covered rooftops and broken walls. Among the rubble, they found the stone wall Leila had mentioned. Sure enough, it bore the same spiral symbol as Daniel's stone.

"This is it!" Daniel said. "But what does it mean?"

As if in answer, Tiko barked and began pawing at the ground near the wall. Beneath a layer of ash, they uncovered a small trapdoor made of metal, rusted but intact. With a bit of effort, they pried it open, revealing a dark tunnel that sloped downward.

"Are we really doing this?" Leila asked, her voice trembling with excitement and fear.

Daniel grinned. "We're already here. Let's see where it goes!"

Chapter 3

Into the Volcano

The tunnel was cool and damp, with walls that glimmered faintly in their flashlight beams. The air smelled of earth and sulfur, a reminder of the volcano's power. As they ventured deeper, the spiral symbol appeared again and again, carved into the walls like a guide.

After what felt like hours, the tunnel opened into a massive underground chamber. The walls were lined with glowing crystals, and at the center of the chamber was a pool of water that shined with a soft, glowing light, almost like it had its own little magic. At the edge of the pool stood an ancient pedestal, and atop it was a large crystal shaped like a spiral.

"It's beautiful," Leila whispered, stepping closer.

Daniel reached out to touch the crystal, but the moment his fingers brushed its surface, the chamber filled with a low rumble. The crystal began to glow brighter, and images appeared in the water—scenes of Montserrat's history, from the island's lush beginnings to the fiery eruptions of Soufrière Hills.

Chapter 4
The Volcano's Secret

The images in the water shifted, showing the volcano once more, but this time it was peaceful. The voice of an elder seemed to echo in the chamber, though no one was there.

"This crystal holds the heart of Montserrat," the voice said. "It is a symbol of balance, a reminder that even the most powerful forces can bring renewal and life. Protect it, and Montserrat will always find harmony."

As the crystal's glow dimmed, the rumbling subsided. Daniel and Leila exchanged awestruck glances. They had discovered a secret that made them feel closer to the island's heart, a sign of strength and hope for Montserrat's future.

Carefully, Daniel and Leila placed the crystal back on the pedestal. "We can't take it," Daniel said. "It belongs here, where it can protect the island."

Leila nodded. "But now we know its secret. That's enough."

Chapter 5
A New Adventure

Back in Salem, Daniel and Leila couldn't stop talking about their discovery. They decided to keep the crystal's location a secret, sharing the story only with a few trusted elders who promised to safeguard the chamber's mystery.

The two friends continued their adventures around Montserrat, their bond strengthened by the incredible journey they had shared. And every time they looked up at Soufrière Hills, they no longer saw it as a threat but as a guardian of their island's history and future.

As for the crystal, it remained hidden deep within the volcano, its spiral symbol a reminder of Montserrat's resilience, its beauty, and the secrets that lie waiting for those brave enough to uncover them.

<u>The End</u>

Collin D. Butler

Story 29:

"The Friendly Whale of Bequia"
Bequia, St. Vincent and the Grenadines

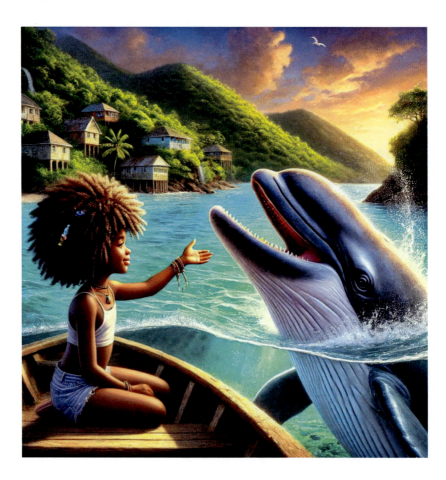

Chapter 1
The Call of the Sea

In the small fishing village of Paget Farm on the island of Bequia, young Zara had always loved the sea. She would sit on the rocky shore, sketching the waves, dreaming of adventures beyond the horizon. Her grandfather, Papa Joe, was a retired fisherman with a heart full of stories about the whales that once graced the island's waters.

"Zara," he said one morning as they walked along the shore, "the sea holds secrets. And sometimes, if you're quiet enough, it will share them with you."

Zara smiled, but she had no idea how true his words would become.

Chapter 2

The Unlikely Encounter

One calm afternoon, Zara borrowed her grandfather's small fishing boat and paddled into Friendship Bay. She was sketching a distant sailboat when she heard a peculiar sound—a low, melodic hum. It echoed through the water, sending shivers up her spine.

Suddenly, a large shape emerged from the deep—a whale with skin as smooth as stone and eyes that seemed to sparkle with curiosity. Zara froze, clutching her sketchpad.

To her amazement, the whale didn't leave. Instead, it swam closer, letting out a series of soft clicks and whistles.

"Hello," Zara whispered, her voice trembling. "Are you... talking to me?"

The whale tilted its massive head as if nodding.

Chapter 3

A Bond Beneath the Waves

For weeks, Zara returned to the bay, where the whale—whom she named Liko—would appear. She brought him gifts: a piece of driftwood, a shiny shell, and even a song she hummed. In return, Liko showed her wonders of the sea: coral gardens, schools of shimmering fish, and hidden coves she had never seen.

Zara shared her adventures with Papa Joe, who smiled knowingly. "Liko must trust you, child. Whales are wise creatures—they sense good hearts."

But not everyone in the village was thrilled. Fishermen complained that Liko was scaring away the fish. "That whale's trouble," grumbled Mr. Byron, a gruff old man. "Best leave it be."

Chapter 4
The Storm and the Struggle

One fateful evening, dark clouds gathered over Bequia. Zara's grandfather warned her to stay ashore, but when she heard Liko's hum over the crashing waves, she couldn't ignore it. She ran to the beach and spotted him trapped near the rocks, tangled in an abandoned fishing net.

Without thinking, Zara paddled out to him. The storm roared around her, and the waves tossed her boat like a toy. "Hold on, Liko!" she shouted, grabbing a knife from the boat's side.

She cut at the net with all her strength, her arms aching as the rain poured down. "You're free, Liko!" she cried as the last strand fell away.

The whale let out a powerful song that seemed to shake the very storm itself. Slowly, the waves calmed, and the rain eased.

Chapter 5
A Hero Returns

By the time Zara and Liko returned to the bay, the entire village had gathered, their lanterns lighting up the shore. Gasps and cheers erupted as Liko swam gracefully around Zara's boat, spraying water into the air like a celebration.

"Zara, you saved him!" cried Papa Joe, pulling her into a hug.

Even Mr. Byron, the gruff fisherman, stepped forward. "That whale's special," he admitted with a nod. "We should protect him—and this bay."

Chapter 6

A New Beginning

From that day forward, the village embraced Liko as part of their community. Fishermen agreed to keep the bay safe from nets and debris, and Zara became a hero, known as the girl who befriended the friendly whale.

Liko continued to visit Zara, often bringing his own gifts—like a shiny piece of coral or a playful nudge that nearly tipped her boat. Together, they reminded everyone of the magic that lay beneath the waves and the importance of protecting the ocean.

Epilogue

As Zara sat with her grandfather one evening, watching the sun set over Friendship Bay, she smiled at the horizon. "The sea really does hold secrets," she said.

Papa Joe chuckled. "And you, my girl, have become one of them."

Liko's song echoed in the distance, a melody that carried the promise of friendship, courage, and the endless mysteries of the sea.

The End

Made in the USA
Columbia, SC
14 June 2025

d5729b01-2ab0-487f-97e7-61442afa6429R02